"Something is bothering you, my son," said Chiun.

Remo nodded. "I think I'm going to be on the wrong side."

Chiun's frail parchment face became puzzled. "Wrong side? What is a wrong side? Will you cease to work for Doctor Smith?"

"Look, you know I can't explain to you who we work for."

"I've never cared," said Chiun. "What difference would it make? You are a pupil of the Master of Sinanju and you perform your assassin's art because that is what you are."

"Dammit, Chiun, I'm an American, and I do what I do for other reasons. And now, they've told me to get up to a peak right away, and I find out I'm going against the good guys."

"Good guys? Bad guys? Are you living in a fairy tale, my son? There are killing points, nerve points, hearts and lungs and eyes and feet and hands and balance. There are no good guys and bad guys. If there were, would armies have to wear uniforms to identify themselves?"

With that, Chiun was silent, but Remo paid no attention to his silence. He was angry, almost as angry as he had been that day a decade before when he had recovered from his public execution, waking up in Folcroft Sanitarium on Long Island Sound. He was angry at the thought of his new assignment.

He had to kill his fellow cops!

The Destroyer #9:
MURDER'S SHIELD

Warren Murphy and Richard Sapir

DESTROYER BOOKS
WARREN MURPHY MEDIA LLC

THE DESTROYER #9: MURDER'S SHIELD

This edition published in 2018 by Destroyer Books/Warren Murphy Media LLC.

ISBN-13: 978-1-944073-29-9

ISBN-10: 1-944073-29-9

Requests for reproduction or interviews should be directed to DestroyerBooks@gmail.com.

Front cover art by Gere Tactical

For Betty Claire, who knows
all there is to do
is what there is to do.

CHAPTER ONE

BIG PEARL WILSON SENT the white fox into the bedroom to get him two handfuls of money. He eased his $185 Gucci slippers into the ankle-high white rug that circled to his bar and around to the drape-covered windows. The drapes were drawn, separating his lush pad from the decaying, teeming Harlem streets — a touch of paradise in Hell. The curtains separating the two were fireproof, somewhat soundproof, and had cost him $2,200. He had paid in cash.

"Have a drink, officer?" said Big Pearl, moving his slow easy majestic way to the bar, the slow and easy way that foxes sniffed.

"No, thank you," said the detective. He looked at his watch.

"A snort?" offered Big Pearl, pointing to his nose.

The detective refused the cocaine.

"I don't snort myself," said Big Pearl. "You waste yourself a little bit every time you use it. These cats on the street live baddest a year, and are broke or dead or forgotten before they see the weather change. They beat on their women and one of 'em talks and it's off to Attica. They think it's a big game with their flashy cars. Me. My women get paid, my cops get paid, my judges get paid, my pols get paid and I make my money. And I've been ten years without a bust."

The girl came bustling back with a manila envelope, unevenly stuffed. Big Pearl gave the insides a condescending glance.

"More," he said. Then he sensed something was wrong. It was the

1

detective. He was on the edge of the deep leather chair and getting up for the package, as if he would be glad to take it with less just to get out of Big Pearl's pad.

"A little extra for you personally," said Big Pearl.

The white detective nodded stiffly.

"You're a new man at headquarters," said Big Pearl. "Usually, they don't send a new man on something like this. Mind if I check with headquarters?"

"No. Go right ahead," said the detective.

Big Pearl smiled his wide, glistening smile. "You know you got the most important job in the whole New York City police department tonight?"

Big Pearl reached under the bar for the telephone. Taped lightly to the inside of the receiver was a small Derringer which slipped neatly and unseen into the palm of his large black hand as he dialed.

"'Lo, Inspector," said Big Pearl, suddenly sounding like a field hand. "This is yo' boy, Big Pearl. Ah got somethin' heah Ah just want to check out. The detective you send down, what he look like?"

Big Pearl stared at the white detective, nodding, saying "Yeah, yeah. Yeah. Yassah. Okay. Much obliged." Big Pearl hung up, returning the Derringer with the phone.

"You white," he said with a big smile, wondering how much of the needle the detective would understand. "You feel all right. You look kind of nervous."

"I'm all right," said the detective. When he had the money, he said, almost as if following orders:

"Who's your contact for Long Island housewives? We know she's a white woman in Great Neck. Who?"

Big Pearl smiled. "You want more money? I'll give you more." It was Big Pearl's cool that enabled him to keep the smile when the white detective drew his .38 Police Special and pointed it at Big Pearl's eyes.

"Hey, man. What's that?"

The white girl gasped and covered her mouth. Big Pearl raised his hands to show there was nothing in them. He wasn't going to try to shoot a cop to protect some paleface in Great Neck. There were other ways, ways that kept you alive.

"Hey, man, I can't give you that stuff. What you need it for anyhow? You New York City. And she pay off in Great Neck."

"I want to know."

"Do you know that if she dry up in Great Neck, the honey machine dry up? No more classy white housewives from Babylon and the Hamptons and all the places where I get my real class. If the honey stop for me, it stop for you. Dig, baby?"

"What's her name?"

"You sure the inspector wants this?"

"*I* want it. You've got three seconds and it better be the right name, Big Pearl, because if it's not, I'm going to come back here and mess up your face and your pad."

"What can I do?" said Big Pearl to the frightened, white chick. "Hey, don't worry, honey. Everything works out. Now, you just stop crying."

Big Pearl waited a second and asked again if the detective wouldn't take, say $3,000.

The detective wouldn't.

"Mrs. Janet Brachdon," said Big Pearl. "Mrs. Janet Brachdon of 811 Cedar Grove Lane, whose husband ain't really all that successful in advertising. Let me know when you shake her down and for how much. 'Cause I don't want her jacking the bill on me. I'm gonna pay it anyhow. You just driving out to Great Neck to get what comes from her anyways."

Big Pearl's tone was heavy-seeded with contempt. Save him from the idiots of the world, Lord, save him from the idiots of the world.

"Janet Brachdon, eight eleven Cedar Grove Lane," repeated the detective.

"Thass right," said Big Pearl.

The gun cracked once and Big Pearl's black face had a hole in it between his eyes. The dark hole filled with blood. The tongue stuck out, and another shot immediately went into the falling face.

"Oh," said the girl weakly, and the detective drilled her in the chest, sending her into a backward somersault. He took two steps to the writhing form of Big Pearl and put a shot into the temple, although the big black pimp was obviously dying. He finished off the girl who was lying clay stiff while her thorax bubbled up red. A shot in the temple also.

He left the apartment. The deep white rug was soaking up great quantities of human blood.

At 8:45 that night, Mrs. Janet Brachdon was serving a roast according to the tenets of Julia Child. The potatoes had not just been mashed; they had been blended with homegrown herbs as Julia had suggested on her television show. Two men, one white and one black, entered the front door and blew Mrs. Brachdon's brains into the blended potatoes as her husband and eldest son looked on. The men apologized to the boy, then shot both the father and son.

In Harrisburg, Pa., a pillar of the community was preparing to address the Chamber of Commerce. His topics were creative financing and how to deal more effectively with the ghetto. His car blew up when he turned on the key. The next day, the local paper received an unusual press release. It was a detailed analysis of how creative the pillar of the community had been.

He could afford to lose money in erecting Hope House for addicts, the news release pointed out. He made enough in heroin sales to absorb the loss.

In Connecticut, a judge who traditionally showed appalling leniency toward people reputed to be members of the Mafia, was taken to his backyard pool by two men with drawn guns. He was asked, under pain of death, to demonstrate his swimming prowess. The request was rather unfair. He had a handicap. His nineteen-inch portable color television set. It was chained to his neck. It was still chained to his neck when the local police department fished him out three hours later.

These deaths, and a half-dozen others, all went to the chairman of a Congressional subcommittee who, one fine bright autumn day, came to the inescapable conclusion that the deaths were not mob warfare. They were something else, something far more sinister. He told the U.S. Attorney General that he intended to launch a Congressional investigation. He asked for the help of the Justice Department. He was assured he would have it. But that did not give him total assurance. Not in his gut.

Outside the Justice Building, in the still, warm Washington Street, Representative Francis X. Duffy of New York City's 13th Congressional District, suddenly remembered the fear he had experienced when he dropped behind the lines in France for the OSS in World War II.

It was his stomach that suddenly lost all feeling and sent the signal to his mind to block out thoughts of anything other than what was around him. Some men lost touch with their surroundings when frightened, and tried to shut out reality. Duffy closed off emotion instead. Which was why he returned from World War II, and some of his colleagues didn't. It was not a virtue that Duffy had perfected. He was born with it, just as he was born with a heart that pumped blood and lungs that took oxygen from the air.

The kind of stomach-rotting fear that most other people experienced came to Francis X. Duffy when he couldn't manage his son, or in a close election, or when his wife went into St. Vincent's Hospital for an operation. That was when his stomach jumped, his palms sweated, and he had to fight for control of himself. Death was another matter.

So here it is, said Frank Duffy's mind. *So here it is coming at you.* He stood before the Justice Building, a fifty-five-year-old man, his fine, neat-combed hair graying, his face lined with the marks of life, his briefcase filled with reports he was sure he would never use. And what amazed him was how well his body remembered to prepare for the possibility of death.

He strolled to a bench. It was speckled with fallen red, yellow, and brown leaves; he brushed them aside. Some youngsters must have spread them there because leaves did not fall that heavy, least of all in Washington in late October.

Things to do before death. The will was all right. Two. Tell Mary Pat that he loved her. Three. Tell his son that life was good and that this was a good country to live it in, maybe the best. Nothing too heavy, though. Maybe just shake his hand and tell him how proud he was of him. Four, confession. That would be necessary, but how could he honestly make his peace with God when he had used methods to have only one child, methods not approved by the Church?

He would have to promise to amend his life, and it seemed dishonest to promise such a thing when the promise didn't mean anything any more. He knew full well that he would not have more children if he could now, so the promise would be a lie. And he did not wish to lie to God, not now.

God had been a problem since his arguments with the sisters at St. Xavier's, extending all the way through the formality of joining the Knights of Columbus because Irish-Catholic politicians from the 13th C.D. all belonged to the Knights of Columbus, just as the Jews sprinkled themselves on hospital boards and social agencies. The religions met at Muscular Dystrophy.

Duffy smiled and breathed the autumn in Washington. He loved this city to the very depth of his being. This crime-ridden brothel on the Potomac where the best hope of mankind still legislated its tortuous way toward a system where people could live safely and justly with other people. Where the son of an Irish bootlegger could rise to congressman and vote with sons of oil millionaires, paupers, farmers, cobblers, racketeers, clergymen, hustlers, and professors. That was America. What the radicals of both the left and right hated about it was its very humanity. They wanted to model America on some abstract purity that had never existed and would never exist. The right with the past; the left with tomorrow.

Duffy looked at his briefcase. In it were reports on the deaths of a pimp, a female recruiter of prostitutes, a heroin dealer, and a judge who had been obviously earning a tidy profit from acquitting people he shouldn't have. And in that briefcase were the signs of great danger to the beautiful country that did exist. America. What to do? The Attorney General had been a good first step, but already it could be dangerous. Could Duffy trust the Justice Department or the FBI? How far had this thing gone? It was big enough to kill a half dozen people already. Was it national? Did it infect the federal agencies? How far and how deep? On that question depended how long he would live. His enemies might not know it yet but they would kill a congressman if need be. They could not stop at anyone now. They had cut themselves free from reality, and now they would destroy what they sought to preserve.

What to do now? Well, a little protection from someone he could trust would do for a starter. The toughest man he knew. Maybe the toughest man in the world. Mean on the outside and mean on the inside.

That afternoon with a pile of change in front of him, Congressman Duffy dialed a long distance number from a pay phone.

"Hello, you lazy sonofabitch, how are you, this is Duffy."

"Are you still alive?" came back the voice. "That candy-ass life you lead should have put you in the grave long before this."

"You'd know on national television or the *New York Times* if I were dead. I'm not a nobody police inspector."

"You wouldn't have the brass for police work, Frankie. You'd only live three minutes with your weepy West Side liberalism."

"Which brings up why I called you, Bill. You don't think I'd just want to say hello."

"No, not a big-shot faggy liberal congressman like you. What do you want, Frankie?"

"I want you to die for me, Bill."

"Okay, just so long as I don't have to listen to your political bullshit. What's up?"

"I think I'm going to be a target very soon. What say we meet at that special place?"

"When?"

"Tonight."

"Okay, I'll leave right away. And Fag-Ass, do me a favor."

"What?"

"Don't get yourself killed before then. They'll make you into another martyr. We got enough of those."

"Just try to read the map without moving your lips, Bill."

Frank Duffy delayed telling his wife he loved her and his son how proud he was of him and God that he was sorry. Inspector William McGurk was another two weeks at least. Guaranteed. Maybe even a natural death.

He drove into Maryland to escape the heavy liquor tax and bought ten quarts of Jack Daniels. Since he would not be stopping at any other stores, he also purchased some soda to go with it.

"A quart," said Congressman Duffy. "A quart of club soda."

The clerk looked at the row of Jack Daniels bottles and said, "You sure a quart's what you want?"

Duffy shook his head.

"You're right. Make it a pint. One of those little bottles."

"We don't have little bottles."

"Then, that's okay. Just what's here on the counter. Hell, make it an even dozen."

"Jack Daniels?"

"What do you think?"

Duffy drove to the airport and loaded the Jack Daniels onto his Cessna, making sure the bottles were flat and even, a central weight on the plane. Not that they would make that much difference, but why take chances? There were old pilots and bold pilots, but no old, bold pilots.

Duffy landed that night in a small private airstrip outside Seneca Falls, New York. A car was waiting. McGurk had driven from New York City. The cold night, the unloading of the plane, and the meeting with McGurk, reminded Duffy of the night in France when he had first met the best weapons man he would ever know. It had been early spring in France and although they knew an invasion would come soon from England, they did not know when or where because high risk people are never given information that the upstairs would not want to see in enemy hands.

It was a weapons drop in Brittany. McGurk and Duffy had been assigned to distribute and teach the use of said weapons in a manner consistent, and with a degree of skill commensurate with, the practical use of such weapons in the field of operations. That is what their secret orders had said.

"We gotta show the frogs how not to blow their feet off when they fire these things," said McGurk.

He was taller than Duffy and his face was surprisingly fleshy for a man so thin, a moon of a face with a button of a nose and rounded soft lips that made him appear about as incisive as a balloon.

Duffy yelled out in French that each man should carry one case and no more. There were three cases left and a young Maquis man tried to hoist one of the extras.

"Bury them," said Duffy in French. "There's no point in your dropping off because you're tired. I'd rather have one case and one man than no case and no man."

The young Maquis still attempted to carry two. McGurk slapped him in the face and pushed him toward the line that was wending its way to the night-shrouded forest near the field.

"You can't explain things to these people," said McGurk. "The only thing they understand is a slap in the face."

In two days, McGurk had taught the French Maquis some basic skills with their new weapons. His instructional method was a slap to get attention, then a demonstration, then another slap if the student failed. To test their proficiency, McGurk asked Duffy to stage a preliminary raid, before the Maquis received their first real combat order. Duffy chose a pass in which to trap a small Nazi convoy that regularly plied its way from a Wehrmacht army base to a major airfield.

The convoy was ambushed at noon. The battle was over in less than three minutes. The French drivers and the German guards came pouring out of the trucks with their hands raised in surrender.

McGurk got them in a line. Then he motioned to the worst marksman among the Maquis. "You. Go fifty yards up that hill. Kill someone."

The young Maquis scrambled up the hill and without catching his breath, fired off a shot. It caught a German guard in the shoulder. The other prisoners fell to the ground, covering their heads with their hands and bringing their knees up into their stomachs. It looked like a road littered with grown fetuses.

"Keep going," McGurk yelled up the hill. "You'll fire until you kill him."

The next shot went wild. The shot after that took out part of a stomach. The next shot after that was wild. The young Maquis was crying.

"I don't want to kill like this," he yelled.

"You kill him or I kill you," said McGurk and raised his carbine to his shoulder, pointing it up the hill. "And I'm no crummy frog marksman. I'll take out your eyes."

Crying, the young Maquis fired again, catching the downed German in the mouth. The head was nearly severed from the neck.

"All right, goosy fingers, you got him," McGurk yelled. He lowered his carbine and turned to another Maquis who had been firing rather poorly in practice. "You're next."

Duffy sidled up to McGurk and said in a hushed voice:

"Bill. Stop this now."

"No."

"Dammit, this is murder."

"That's very right, Frankie. Now button your lip, or I'll put you in the shooting line too."

The German guards were dispatched in short order and only the French drivers were left. McGurk waved another Maquis up the hill. He refused to go.

"I will not kill Frenchmen," he said.

"I don't see how you little shits could tell the difference if it wasn't for the uniforms," said McGurk.

Suddenly, a Maquis standing nearby raised his carbine and walked it into McGurk's lean stomach.

"We will not kill Frenchmen."

"Okay," said McGurk. A sudden broad grin appeared. "Have it your own way. I was just testing you."

"We are now tested and you know we won't kill Frenchmen like dogs."

"Hey, I didn't mean to be too rough on you. Hell, it's war," said McGurk warmly. He draped an arm over the Maquis as the carbine lowered. "Friends?" he said.

"Friends," said the Frenchman.

McGurk shook hands and scrambled up the hill, pushing an angry Frank Duffy before him. Eight seconds later, the Maquis with the carbine was cut in half by the explosion of a grenade on his belt. McGurk had pulled the pin when he embraced him. From the top of the hill, McGurk unloaded his carbine at the French truck drivers who were still curled on the road. Bam. Bam. Bam. Heads exploded. No misses. There was quiet on the noon road as the bodies lay motionless; the Maquis band looked up in terror at this maniac American.

"All right, let's pull out," yelled McGurk.

That night, when McGurk was bedding down, Duffy threw a punch at his head, knocking McGurk into a wall. McGurk bounded back and Duffy caught him with a knee, square in his moon face. McGurk shook his head.

"What was that for?" he asked.

"Because you're a sonofabitch," said Duffy.

"You mean because of shooting the prisoners?"

"Yes."

"You know, as your leader, I could have you shot right now with incredible justification?"

Duffy shrugged. He didn't plan on living through the war anyway. McGurk must have sensed this, because he said, "Okay, we'll go cleaner in the future. Hell, I don't want to kill an American." McGurk staggered to his feet and offered his hand.

As Duffy reached forward for it, he kept going into McGurk's stomach. McGurk emitted a gasp. He backed away, putting his hands in front of him.

"Hey, hey, I meant it, friend. I gotta have *someone* I can't kill. Now, stop it."

"You can't take it, can you?" Duffy said arrogantly.

"Can't take it? Kid, I could wipe you up in a second. Believe me. Just don't come at me again. That's all I ask."

Either from youthful wildness or contempt, Duffy went for McGurk again. He remembered throwing one punch and he awoke with McGurk pouring water on his face.

"I told you I could take you, kid. How do you feel?"

"I don't know," said Duffy, blinking. Throughout the war, Duffy remained the one person McGurk could not kill. Despite logic and moral training, a deep affection grew in Frank Duffy for Bill McGurk, the man who could not kill him. He came to look upon McGurk's cold passion for death as a sickness and, as with any friend who was sick, he felt sorry for him; he didn't hate him for it.

Duffy became wary of picking up slights from anyone, lest McGurk find out about it and shred the person. After the war, it was the same way. When Frank Duffy was running for assemblyman, some hecklers began shaking the speakers' platform. McGurk, then a uniformed sergeant in the police department, formally arrested the offenders for disturbing the peace. Later, they were also charged with assaulting a police officer. On the way to the station house, out of sight of the political rally, the offenders did attempt with hand and fist to strike Officer McGurk about the head. The offenders were admitted to Beth Israel Hospital with fractures of the cranium, facial contusions, and hernias. McGurk was treated for bruised knuckles. McGurk was godfather to Duffy's boy. The two families even managed to get along well enough to share a cabin outside Seneca Falls, New York, where Duffy on this early autumn evening had landed with the dozen bottles of Jack Daniels and a very big problem.

Driving to the cabin in the stillness of the dark country road, the United States congressman opened one of the bottles, took a swig and passed it to the Inspector in charge of Manpower Deployment for the New York City Police Department. McGurk took a swig and passed it back to Duffy.

"I don't know where to begin, Bill," said Duffy. "It's monstrous. On the surface, it looks like a benefit to the nation but when you understand what's happening, you realize it is an incredible danger to everything America stands for."

"Communists?"

"No. Although they're a danger too. No. These people are like Communists. They believe the end justifies any means."

"Sure as hell does, Frankie," said McGurk.

"Bill, I need your help, not your political philosophy, if you don't mind. What's happening is this. A group of people are taking the law into their own hands. Massive vigilantes. Very thorough, almost military. Like those police in South America a few years ago. Trying to fight liberal politicians and lenient judges with bullets."

"Judges here are too lenient," McGurk said. "Why do you think decent citizens can't walk the streets? The animals have taken over. New York City is a jungle. Your district too. You ought to go down and talk to your constituents some time, Frankie. You'll find them hiding in their caves."

"Come on, Bill, let me finish."

"You let *me* finish," McGurk said. "We opened the doors to the ape house in New York and now decent people venture onto the streets at their own risk."

"I'm not going to argue politics or try to cure your racism, Bill. But let me finish. I think policemen are doing the same thing in America now that they were doing in South America a couple of years ago. I think they're organized."

"You got an informer?" asked McGurk. He took the bottle as he turned onto a dirt driveway. The car bounced over the dirt road as

McGurk refused to be intimidated by the narrowness and unevenness of its surface.

"No," Duffy said.

"Then why do you think police are doing it?"

"Good question. Who's getting killed? The people that the policemen ordinarily can't touch. I recognized the name of Elijah Wilson. You told me about Big Pearl yourself. Remember years ago, you said the law couldn't touch him?"

"Yeah. Everybody knows Big Pearl."

"Everybody in *your* business, not in mine. Well, that got me thinking. Even a racist like you admits that a man like Big Pearl is smart. He doesn't put himself in a position where he's going to be killed. The average pimp lasts two years. He was going for fifteen. How? By making it profitable for people not to kill him. So the motive had to be something other than profit, right?"

"If you say so, Sherlock," said McGurk.

"Okay. Then we get the financier in Harrisburg, Pennsylvania. Maybe he made enemies. In heroin, that's possible."

"Right."

"But he operated like Big Pearl. He paid. And made it unprofitable to kill him. And the judge in Connecticut was another one on the take. His life was very profitable to the Mafia."

"Maybe he took and didn't deliver," said McGurk. He wheeled the car sharply into the darkness and stopped. He turned off the lights and an outline of a small cabin could be seen from the car.

Duffy grabbed two bottles and McGurk grabbed two bottles and they stepped gingerly over the rock-strewn earth to the cabin entrance. McGurk turned on the lights and Duffy got the ice.

"You look at the judge's record," Duffy said. "He always delivered. The Mafia had a good reason to keep him alive."

"Okay. It wasn't the mob. Maybe it was some nut." McGurk twisted the plastic ice cube tray, sending ice skittering across the Formica tabletop. He gathered handfuls of the ice and filled two large mugs Duffy brought forth.

"Nuts don't work that well," Duffy said. "I know that. Fill the tray. We're going to be out of ice soon if you don't."

"Oswald didn't work that well. Sirhan Sirhan didn't work that well.

There are two dead Kennedys because of nuts who didn't work well. I'll fill a couple on the next tray."

"Those were one-hit affairs, Bill. These things aren't. There's a string of them. Bam. Bam. Bam. They get in. They get out. Over and over. That's not nuts; that's competence any way you want to slice it. Fill the tray now."

McGurk raised his mug and smiled.

"To two dumb donkeys — us," he said.

"To two dumb donkeys — us," said Duffy.

They clinked mugs and drank and walked into the living room, letting the remaining ice cubes melt in the tray.

"I'd have two choices for who's doing these killings," said Duffy. "Soldiers or cops. Somebody professional."

"Okay, soldiers or cops," said McGurk.

"Cops," said Duffy. "Soldiers couldn't find their rectums if not located near toilet seats."

McGurk smiled broadly.

"Okay, cops. Why haven't there been identifications? Cops' faces are known around their cities, especially in cities under a half-million."

Duffy leaned forward on the torn leather couch. His face broke into a grin, one former professional making judgment on current professionals.

"That's the beauty of it. I figure it's reciprocal hits." He put his mug down on the wooden floor and reinforced his explanation with his hands. He put them out wide to either side, then crossed them to the far sides. "New York cops make a hit in Harrisburg. Harrisburg makes a hit in Connecticut. Connecticut cops make a hit in New York or what have you. The locals set it up; the outsiders hit. It's foolproof. You know the hardest thing in an assigned hit is finding the sonofabitch of a target. If it weren't for the Maquis that knew France, we couldn't have found our way into Paris."

McGurk shook his head.

"You Fordham guys were always so fucking smart. We could always tell a Fordham guy. He read books."

"So what do you think?" asked Duffy.

"I think you're right. What do *you* have to do with this?"

"I'm going to be on the list for hits soon. I don't want to die."

McGurk looked puzzled. "Frankie, you're a congressman. An honest congressman. We've been talking about the scum of the earth. Pimps. Heroin financiers. Whore recruiters. Crooked judges. Mafiosi button men. Where does that come up to you? Where does that even come close to you? What the hell is the matter with you, Frankie?" McGurk's voice became throbbing angry, a pleading disgust. "Look at the facts, dammit. You're not some cock-a-doodle-doo broad out of a consciousness-raising session where they come in looking to jerk themselves off. You're a liberal but you think. You deal in facts. But this time, you've got nothing. No facts. You might as well be out in a street screaming slogans. Stop the killing. Stop the killing. Stop the killing." McGurk's voice hit the rhythm of the streets, the mindless chanting of demonstrators. But there was no smile on Duffy's face, as McGurk had expected when he made a good point. Suddenly, surprisingly, there were tears and Frank Duffy was crying for the first time in McGurk's memory.

"Oh, Jesus," said Frank Duffy and lowered his head to his hands.

"Hey, Frank, what's wrong? C'mon, stop that. Stop that, will you? C'mon," said McGurk. He comforted his friend with his arm.

"Oh, Jesus, Bill," said Duffy.

"What's the matter, dammit? What's the matter?"

"Mafiosi button man is the matter."

"Yeah?"

"I never mentioned Mafiosi button men. I never mentioned one. So you killed him, too. You had your people kill him too."

McGurk threw his mug across the room where it shattered against the pine wall with a splat. He rose in anger, punching the palm of his hand.

"Why do you have to be so smart? Why do you Fordham guys have to be so frigging smart? Frankie, why do you have to be so smart?"

Duffy saw the ice cubes and water begin to stain the wooden floor. He rose and tapped McGurk on the back.

McGurk jumped, then said, "Oh," when he saw the offer of Duffy's mug.

"What are we going to do?" asked Duffy.

"I'll tell you what we're going to do, smart Fordham guy. You stop your investigation and if any of the people come near you, I'll powder them like sugar cubes is what we're gonna do."

"You knew about the investigation?"

"And other things. We're good and we're growing. We're gonna give this country back to the decent people. The hard-working people. The honest people. This country has been turning into a cesspool long enough. We're just gonna get rid of the crap."

"Impossible, Bill, you can't do it. Because you start with crap and then you move onto anyone else who gets in your way. What's going to be the check on you? What happens when your people start taking money to miss? Or start free-lancing?"

"We'll take care of them too."

"It's the we who'll be doing it, and who's to stop them?"

"If that happens, I'll turn on them."

"No, you won't. You'll be too happy doing what you love best."

"And you might even be president then. Did you ever think of that?"

Duffy took back his drink. "We have any ice left?"

"Yeah. Plenty. Plenty."

"Okay, I'll get some more. Look, I want to phone Mary Pat and tell her goodbye and…uh, I want to say goodbye to my son. I don't imagine you'll let me reach a priest."

"What is this talk?" said McGurk angrily.

"You're going to get orders to kill me tonight. You left word where you can be reached?"

"Not at the department."

"No. With your real boss. Whoever you're really working for now. He couldn't let his killer arm go wandering around out of touch for any length of time. You *are* the killer arm?"

"That's right. So what do you have to worry about? You're the one person I can't kill. You're golden, sweetheart."

"I'm dead, Bill. Dead meat."

"Okay, dead meat. We may have some frozen hamburgers. You want one?"

"No."

They drank in silence as the hamburgers sizzled. A few times, McGurk attempted jokes. "How does it feel to be dead?" or "Wow, are you lucky. I haven't killed you for five minutes."

The phone rang, a ting-a-ling upstate ring so strange to people from New York City.

"It's for you, Bill. It's your boss," said Duffy without rising.

The phone continued to ring.

"If it isn't my boss, will you relax?"

Duffy smiled. "They're the only ones who know you're up here. No one knows where *I* am. So it's them. And they're going to tell you to kill me. Probably make it look like a suicide to discredit my investigation."

McGurk laughed. "Why should I even answer the phone? You know everything."

His hand was on the phone and he lifted it to his ear. He was still smiling as he said, "Yes, yes, yes." And, "Are you sure?" But the smile was different at the end of the call. It had become a mask.

"How you fixed for another drink?" asked McGurk.

"I'll get it. You never fill the ice cube tray," said Duffy.

In the kitchen, he opened the refrigerator door. Using that as a shield, he eased open the kitchen door, and slid out, onto the gravel; then he was running to the car. He didn't make it. He was tackled from behind and before he could get his hand around to ward off any blows, he slipped into deep darkness, realizing that at last he was paying the final price for tolerating McGurk's brutality for so long.

On his way to the last sleep, a strange thing appeared to Duffy's mind. It was a vision; he was told that he would be forgiven his transgressions and given the reward of a good life. And in that brief moment at the threshold of dark eternity, he was told that a force of nature would take up standards against his killers and that from the depth of human strength would be unleashed a terrible shattering force.

And then the brief moment was over.

CHAPTER TWO

HIS NAME WAS REMO and as he stood on the platform high in the darkened tent, he felt that his body was one with the forces of nature and he was the depth of all human strength.

The animal smells of the empty arena below were strong eighty feet above the sawdust. The outside breeze slapped at the tent. It was cold in that little high pocket where he stood and the swinging bar felt cold as death under his hands as he flipped it back in a long smooth arc.

"Has he done it yet?" said someone down below.

"You have not been paid to witness but to provide this area which you are not using now. Begone," responded a squeaky Oriental voice below.

"But there are no safety nets."

"You were not asked to supervise safety," came the creaky Oriental voice.

"But I gotta see this. There's no lights up there. He's at the top of the high trapeze with no lights."

"One finds seeing things difficult when one's face is buried in the ground."

"Are you trying to threaten me, Pops? C'mon, old man."

Remo stopped the bar. He yelled down to the cavernous arena.

"Chiun. Leave him alone. And you, buddy, if you don't get out of here, you don't get paid."

"What's it any skin off your nose? You're committing suicide anyway. Besides, I already got my money."

"Look," yelled Remo. "Just get away from that little old man. Please."

"The noble elderly gentleman with the wise eyes," added Chiun, lest the circus owner be confused by Remo's description.

"I ain't botherin' no one."

"You are bothering me," said Chiun.

"Well, Pops, that's the way it goes. I'm sitting down right here."

Suddenly there was a piercing scream at the floor of the tent. Remo saw a large balloon of a figure pitch forward and land on its face. It did not move.

"Chiun. That guy just wanted to sit down. You better not have done anything serious."

"When one removes garbage, one does not do anything serious."

"He'd better be alive."

"He never was alive. I could smell hamburger meat on his foul breath. You could smell the meat miles away. He was not alive."

"Well, his heart better be beating."

"It's beating," came the response from below. "And I am aging, waiting to see the simplest of skills, the meager accomplishments of my great and intense years of training, some small proof that the best years of my life have not been wasted on a dullard."

"I mean beating so that he will wake up, not just the twitching of a stiff."

"Do you wish to come down here and kiss him?"

"All right, all right."

"And let us attempt decent form this time, please."

Remo threw the bar out. He knew that Chiun could see him as if stage lights flooded the darkness at the top of the tent. The eye was a muscle and to see in darkness was only an adjustment of that muscle, which could be trained as any other muscle could. It was almost a decade before that Chiun had first told him this, told him that most men go to the grave using less than ten per cent of their skills, muscles, coordination and nerves. "One must only look at the grasshopper," Chiun had said, "or the ant to see energy properly used. Man has forgotten this use. I will remind you."

Remind him he had, in years of training that had more than once brought Remo to the threshold of mind-shattering pain, past the limits of what he had thought a human body could do. And always there were new limits.

"Get on with it," came Chiun's voice.

Remo caught the bar and threw it again. He felt its presence swing out across the tent. Then his body took over. The toes flipped and the hands were forward and he was in space, rising to the apex before the fall, and at the apex, the bar which his senses perceived in the darkness was there in his hands. Up he swung, flipping his body in somersaults just above the swinging bar within the frame of the two wires holding the bar. One. Two.

Three. Four. Then catch the bar with the knees and balance. Hands at sides, knees on bar swinging backward, again to the apex and then, like a chess piece, topple backward, free of the bar, free of any support, falling, down to the sawdust, a lead force dropping to earth, and no movement, head first, not a muscle moving, not even a vagrant thought in the mind. Bang. The cat-fast center of the body forward, feet out, catch the ground, go down to it, perfect even decompression.

On the feet, stand up straight, weight perfectly balanced.

"Perfect," thought Remo. "I was perfect this time. Even Chiun must admit it. As good as any Korean ever. As good as good Chiun, because his was perfection."

Remo strolled over to the aged Korean in the flowing white, golden-bordered robe.

"I think it came off fairly well," Remo said with feigned casualness.

"What?" said Chiun.

"The World Series. What do you think I was talking about?" said Remo.

"Oh, that," said Chiun.

"That," said Remo.

"That was proof that if you have someone of the quality of the Master of Sinanju, you can get a reasonable performance occasionally. Even from a white man."

"Reasonable?" Remo yelled. "Reasonable? That was perfect. That was perfection and I did it. If it wasn't perfect, what was wrong? Tell me, what was wrong?"

"It's chilly in here. Let us go."

"Name one thing any Master of Sinanju could have done better."

"Show less pride because pride is flaw."

"I mean, up on the bar," Remo persisted.

"I see our friend is moving. See how well I kept my promise on his staying alive?"

"Chiun, admit it. Perfection."

"Does my saying perfection make it perfection? If that is required, then the act itself was less than perfection. Therefore," said Chiun with a high happy note in his voice, "I must say that it was less than perfect."

The circus owner groaned and rose to his feet.

"What happened?" he asked.

"I decided not to try any tricks in the dark and climbed down," Remo said.

"You ain't getting your money back. You rented the place. If you didn't do your tricks, it ain't my fault. Anyway, you're lucky. Nobody ever did a four-somersault. Nobody."

"I guess you're right," Remo said.

The circus owner shook his head. "What happened to me?"

"One of your seats collapsed," said Remo.

"Where? Which one? They look good to me."

"This one over here," said Remo, touching the metal bottom of the seat nearest to Chiun.

When the circus owner saw the crack appear before his eyes, he attributed it to the fall he had taken. Otherwise he would have had to believe that this nut who'd chickened out on the high-wire tricks, had actually cracked the bottom of a metal seat with his hand. And he wasn't about to believe that of anyone.

Remo put on his street clothes over his dark tights, a pair of flared blue flannel pants and a clean blue shirt with just enough collar not to appear stodgy. His dark hair was trimmed short and his angular features were handsome enough to belong to a movie star. But the dark eyes said that this was not a movie star. The eyes did not communicate; they absorbed, and looking into them gave some people the uneasy feeling of staring into a cave. He was of average build and only his thick wrists belied any superior strength.

"Didja forget your wristwatch?" asked the circus owner.

"No," said Remo. "I don't wear one any more."

21

"Too bad," said the owner. "Mine's broken and I've got an appointment."

"It's three forty-seven and thirty seconds," said Remo and Chiun in unison. The owner looked puzzled.

"You guys are kidding, right?"

"Right," said Remo.

Seconds later, outside the tent, the owner was surprised to find that the time was three forty-eight. But the two men were not around to be asked how they could tell time without wristwatches. They were in a car on their way to a motel room on the outskirts of Fort Worth, Texas, zipping along a highway strewn with beer cans and the bodies of dogs — the victims of Texas drivers who believe head-on collisions are just another form of brakes.

"Something is bothering you, my son," said Chiun.

Remo nodded. "I think I'm going to be on the wrong side."

Chiun's frail parchment face became puzzled.

"Wrong side?"

"Yes, I think I'm going in on the wrong side this time." His voice was glum.

"What is a wrong side? Will you cease to work for Doctor Smith?"

"Look, you know I can't explain to you who we work for."

"I've never cared," said Chiun. "What difference would it make?"

"It does make a difference, dammit. Why do you think I do what I do?"

"Because you are a pupil of the Master of Sinanju and you perform your assassin's art because that is what you are. The flower gives to the bee and the bee makes honey. The river flows and mountains sit content and sometimes rumble. Each is what he is. And you, Remo, are a student in the House of Sinanju despite the fact that you are white."

"Dammit, Chiun, I'm an American, and I do what I do for other reasons. And now, they've told me to get up to a peak right away, and then I find out I'm going in against the good guys."

"Good guys? Bad guys? Are you living in a fairy tale, my son? You sound like the little children yelling things in the street or your president on the picture box. Have you not learned of our teaching? Good guys, bad guys! There are killing points, nerve points, hearts and lungs and eyes and feet and hands and balance. There are no good guys and bad guys. If there were, would armies have to wear uniforms to identify themselves?"

"You wouldn't understand, Chiun."

"I understand that the poor of the village of Sinanju eat, because the Master of Sinanju serves a master who pays. The food of one tastes just as sweet as the food of another. It is food. You have not learned fully, but you will." Chiun shook his head sadly. "I have given you perfection, as you demonstrated this afternoon, and now you act like a white man."

"So you admit it was perfect?"

"What good is perfection in the hands of a fool? It is a precious emerald buried in a dung heap."

And with that, Chiun was silent, but Remo paid no attention to his silence. He was angry, almost as angry as he had been that day a decade before when he had recovered from his public execution, waking up in Folcroft Sanitarium on Long Island Sound.

Remo Williams had been framed for a murder he did not commit, and then publicly executed in an electric chair that did not work. When he recovered, they told him that they had needed a man who did not exist to act as the killer arm for an agency set up outside the U.S. Constitution to preserve that Constitution from organized crime, revolutionaries, and from all who would overthrow the nation. The crime-fighting organization was CURE, and only four men knew of it: The President of the United States, Dr. Harold Smith, head of CURE, the recruiter, and now Remo. And the recruiter had killed himself to prevent himself from talking, telling Remo that "America is worth a life." Then there were only three who knew.

That was the moment when Remo decided to take the job. And for a decade, he thought he had long since buried the Remo Williams he used to be — a simple, foot-slogging patrolman on the Newark police force. It was so long ago that he had been a cop; and that cop had died in the electric chair.

So Remo had thought...until now. But now he realized that the policeman had not died in the electric chair. Patrolman Remo Williams still lived. His stomach told him. It was churning at the thought of his new assignment; having to kill fellow cops.

CHAPTER THREE

THERE WAS SOME QUESTION WHETHER Representative Francis X. Duffy, D-13th C.D., N.Y., could be buried in Church-sanctified ground. Suicides were not welcomed in holy ground, for to take one's own life was a grave offense against God who had given that life.

Yet, in the strictness of the Church was a humble demand for accuracy, a realistic knowledge of the limitations of man's perceptions. What served as proof to the police department of Seneca Falls, N.Y., and the national news media, was hardly sufficient for the Church.

There were powder burns on Francis Duffy's temple. The paraffin test showed that *his* finger had pulled the trigger. The police said the bruises occurred when he fell. He had been despondent and drinking heavily. His closest friend, Inspector William McGurk of the New York City police department, told the Church in confidence that his friend had been drinking secretly for over a year, very heavily. He had become more paranoid as alcoholism progressed. McGurk also told this to the U.S. Attorney General who had asked that he keep their meeting quiet.

"Did he tell you about a suspected conspiracy?" asked the U.S. Attorney General.

"Conspiracy?" asked McGurk, lifting an eyebrow in his round moon face.

"Yes, conspiracy."

"Which one?"

"You tell me, Inspector."

"Okay, he said the police were banding together to execute criminals and they were going to get him next because he knew about it. Farmers planned to burn him alive in his home because he was going to prove farm parity was a plot by Protestants to hurt Catholics. The Knights of Columbus had been taken over by the Mafia. The United Jewish Appeal had gained secret control over Alcoholics Anonymous in order to ruin the liquor industry or something, and that was why he couldn't go to A.A. There was the doorman in his New York apartment building who reported on his empty bottles and was working for his political opponent. Sir, this is very unpleasant. Frank Duffy was my closest friend."

"Let's talk about the police conspiracy, Inspector. What do you know about it?"

"That he had launched an investigation."

"Did he give you any details?"

"Yes. He had details for everything. It frightened me."

"Why?"

"Because he almost had me believing it."

"Tell me why you almost believed it, Inspector."

"Well, he listed a lot of deaths of underworld figures. And I knew one of them, Big Pearl Wilson. A ni...black pimp. Very cool. Very smart. I mean, there are a lot of intelligent black people."

"Yes, of course, go on."

"Well, Big Pearl took care of people if you know what I mean. Heavy vig. That means..."

"I know the terms of New York corruption," the Attorney General said in a dry Arizona voice. "Go on."

"Well, who would want to kill Big Pearl? He was careful, smart. The cop theory really made sense."

"Excuse me, Inspector, Congressman Duffy told me he shared this information with no one. How did you get it?"

McGurk smiled. "I'm his closest friend. He didn't consider me someone."

The Attorney General nodded. His face was pitted like the drying desert after a hail storm.

"About Big Pearl Wilson. Why *you* think he was killed?"

"I don't know. That's why I say the conspiracy theory almost seemed to make sense. Look. I don't know if you're allowed to do things like this but if you want, I'll take a look into Big Pearl myself. To see if Frankie might have had something."

The Attorney General pondered the offer. "Maybe," he said. "Maybe Congressman Duffy was paranoid when he took his own life. Maybe he didn't take his own life. I don't know. But his story had that ring of truth to it. Do you know what I mean?"

McGurk nodded. "I almost believed it too, and this was after the doorman, the farmers, the UJA and the Knights of Columbus."

"If Duffy was right, of all the police officers in the United States, you're the only one I can be sure is not involved."

McGurk cocked an eyebrow. "How can you be sure? You just don't know."

"I know. I've seen your records. I had you checked out. McGurk, they had notes in old OSS files that it was risky to send you and Duffy on missions together because you were too protective of him. I know you're a rock-ribbed conservative. Duffy was a liberal. Yet, you two were like this," said the Attorney General, squeezing two fingers together airtight. "Like this. Only a deep friendship can consider deep political convictions irrelevant. I know. And if you were in this conspiracy, if there is a conspiracy, well, I know Frank Duffy would be alive today."

McGurk swallowed. "I wish there *were* something like a police conspiracy. I wish there was someone who had killed him. Because then I could skin that scumbag alive. I mean it."

"Calm down, McGurk. I'm not issuing license for murder. But I want you to walk with me a very hard mile."

"Name it."

"Let's assume a conspiracy exists. I want you to check out Big Pearl's death quietly but completely. If there's a conspiracy and you're found out, you'll be killed. Will you do it?"

"For Frank Duffy, sir, I would die."

"You may have to, Inspector." The Attorney General wrote down a telephone number. "Private. Leave no messages with my secretary."

"Right, sir."

"And Inspector. Let's hope that everything Duffy imagined was the result of alcoholic paranoia, because your life isn't worth a coyote's poop if Duffy was right about this."

McGurk's moon face broke into a slashing grin.

"Why, you shit-kicking farmer, everything after World War II was gravy anyhow."

The Attorney General laughed and offered his hand. McGurk took it.

Funny, thought the Attorney General, a man of such honesty and courage has the cold grip of a liar. Well, that disproved another Western saying: that you could tell a man by his handshake.

The President, reviewing the confrontation that evening, was not impressed by the Attorney General's actions.

"Dammit, you're not setting up a special police force in this administration. There are enough cuckoos running around here playing secret agent and I have to clean up after them. That goes for you. That goes for everyone."

"I think, Mr. President, that you're being unreasonable in the face of such a clear and present danger."

"I'm being President of the United States. Our nation is sustained by laws. We will live within them."

"Sir, we're dealing with something the law can't handle."

"Well, it's almost three-hundred years too late for that, isn't it?"

"You mean the Constitution, don't you?"

"I mean America. Good night. If you want to put that New York City policeman on your payroll, all right. But no secret people, secret vendettas, and secret espionage."

"Yes, sir," said the Attorney General. "Although an organization like that might not be a bad idea."

"Good night," said the President. When the Attorney General had left the oval office, the President solemnly made his way through the White House to his bedroom. His wife was napping and he asked her apologetically to leave. She was a good trooper and she understood. A wife like her was a blessing greater than rubies. Old Testament. They must have had her in mind when they wrote the Good Book.

In the top bureau drawer was the red phone. He dialed. The phone rang once.

"Yes, sir," came the voice.

27

WARREN MURPHY & RICHARD SAPIR

"Doctor Smith, there are some worrisome things happening. I am wondering if you people have not overstepped your bounds."

"Are you referring to the executions in the East?"

"Yes. This sort of thing cannot be tolerated. Operating with discretion, your organization is intolerable enough. Running amok, it must be stopped."

"That's not us, Mr. President. That's someone else. We are on it."

"It wasn't you, then?"

"Of course not. We don't have an army, sir. And that sort of sloppiness would never be tolerated by our person. We are moving against whoever is responsible."

"You are going to use that person, then?"

"If we can."

"What do you mean?"

"I cannot elaborate."

The President paused, looking at the red phone. Finally, he said, "For now, you may continue. But I think you should know I do not rest easier knowing you exist."

"Neither do I, sir. Good night."

In a motel outside Fort Worth, the customer in Room 12 had a message from his aunt. The room clerk trudged wearily to the door and knocked. The door opened and a voice said, "Yes?"

"It's a telegram for you."

"Who's it from?"

"I don't know."

"Read it."

"Well, okay. It's from your Aunt Harriet in Minneapolis."

"Thanks," came the voice and the door shut in the clerk's face. He blinked, startled, then knocked again.

"Hey, do you want this telegram or don't you?"

"No," came the voice.

"What?"

"I don't want it. You ever get a telegram you didn't want?"

"Ah'll be a toad's tail," said the clerk, scratching his head.

"Fine," came the voice from inside.

When the clerk left, Remo packed his last sock. He pushed it roughly into the corner of the suitcase. Chiun watched him.

"I am worried," said Chiun.

"About what?" said Remo brusquely.

"There are enough people who will try to kill you. Why must you make their job easier by carrying the shackles of anger?"

"Because I'm mad is why. That telegram was the signal. And I'm going in and I don't want to go in."

"I give you this advice. Of all the people you will see, none is worth the giving of your life."

"My life, my life. It's my life, dammit, and I have a right to piss it away if I feel like it. It's not your life. It's not Smith's life. It's mine. Even though the bastards took it away from me ten years ago. Mine."

Chiun shook his head sadly.

"You carry the wisdom of the pain of my ancestors of Sinanju. Do not destroy it for boyish thoughts."

"Let's put it where it's at, Little Father. You got paid to teach me. Cold, hard, American taxpayer cash. You would have taught a giraffe to kill for a price."

"Do you really think I would have taught you all that I have taught you for money?"

"I don't know. Are you packed?"

"You know. You do not wish to admit it."

"And you aren't all that concerned solely with the idea of wasting a few years of your life. Admit that, too."

"The Master of Sinanju does not admit. He illuminates."

Remo snapped the luggage shut. When Chiun did not wish to talk, Chiun did not talk.

CHAPTER FOUR

In philadelphia, stefano colosimo was greeting his children and grandchildren and his brothers and sisters and cousins, kissing both male and female alike on the cheek in the gusty love of a patriarch for his family.

In small happy groups they came to greet Grandpa Stefano, moving through the foyer past the bodyguards, to feel the heavy hands and the wet lips, and then to get the little brightly-wrapped packages. For the children, it would be cakes and toys. For the grownups, there was jewelry and sometimes an envelope if family finances were not going well. Grandpa Stefano would give these envelopes with heartfelt respect, mentioning that it was only undeserved good fortune that enabled him to do this small thing for a relative and, who knows, perhaps the relative would be able to do him a favor some day too.

The bodyguards, their faces like stone, marked a severe contrast to the joyful family reunion. But then, no one paid attention to bodyguards any more than one paid attention to plumbing.

Some of the younger Colosimos, when they went to school, were surprised to discover that their classmates did not have bodyguards. Some had maids, some even had chauffeurs, but none had bodyguards. And it was then that the children got the first inkling of what it meant to be a Colosimo. You didn't tell everything in classroom show-and-tell. You were in the class but not part of it. The people they talked about on the television news, you had heard on the telephone asking to speak to your grandpa. And you kept this very quiet in class because you were a Colosimo.

Grandpa Colosimo greeted his family and received respect from the outside world also. There were messages and calls from the mayor, a senator, the governor, every city councilman, the chief of police, and the state chairmen of the Democratic and Republican parties. All wishing Philadelphia's largest builder, olive oil importer, and real estate developer a very happy fortieth wedding anniversary.

So it was laughable when the lowly patrolman became insistent that a car outside was blocking the street and he wished to speak to the owner of the house.

"Carlo, take care of it," Grandpa Stefano said to one of his bodyguards.

"He says he wants to speak only to the owner," said Carlo Digibiassi whose income tax returns listed him as a business consultant.

"Take care of him, Carlo," said Grandpa Stefano, rubbing a thumb across the tips of his fingers to indicate small bills.

The bodyguard disappeared into the happy throng, then returned, shrugging his shoulders.

"What kind of a cop is this?" he asked.

"Did you tell him we know people?"

Carlo nodded, exaggeratedly, indicating he had not only told but had been rebuffed.

"Tell him we'll take his ticket."

"He says it's an ordinance. He can take you in."

"For parking?"

Carlo shrugged.

"See who he is, this policeman," said Grandpa Stefano. The order launched phone calls to headquarters, to precincts, to policemen who were employees of Colosimo although they were never carried on company books.

Carlo returned. "Headquarters knows him, but some of our people say they never heard of him."

With the resignation of a man who realizes he must handle

everything himself, Grandpa Stefano went outside to speak to the policeman.

On his porch, flanked by bodyguards, he introduced himself. "Can I be of any help?" he said.

"Yeah. That car out there. It's a vehicular hazard."

"On my wedding anniversary?"

"Sorry. A vehicular hazard is a vehicular hazard."

"A vehicular hazard," said Grandpa Stefano with just a hint of contempt in his voice. "No one else can move this vehicular hazard. All right. I will go."

On the curb, Carlo noticed something unusual. It was not the four other policemen coming toward them. It was the way they came. Like a basketball team with the two tall front men setting picks for the two shorter men behind, as if they would jump up to take a shot. They did not jump up, however; they shot from the hip. The flash was the last thing Carlo saw.

The five policemen drew their guns simultaneously. All went for the bodyguards. For a flash of a moment, only one man stood unscathed, and that was Grandpa Stefano Colosimo and then he was cut down by all five guns.

The bulletin made the 2:00 p.m. news. Philadelphia police were blaming the killing on a rival gang faction.

In New York City, Inspector William McGurk flipped off his radio and scribbled some numbers on a yellow pad. Very neat. It took five men and that was a lot, but it was worth it. Very neat, indeed.

McGurk leaned back in his chair and locked his eyes on the map on the wall of his office in police headquarters, across the hall from the commissioner's. He could visualize the web of policemen moving farther and farther across the country. He had done a great deal already. And now his papers were in; any day now his retirement as the police department's manpower deployment officer would become effective, and he could spend full time on his other, more important, mission. And then that web would expand. With a blooded army, it would travel west, and north and south. Texas. California. Chicago. Ultimately, of course there was Washington. There would always be Washington. And Duffy, with his Fordham cleverness, had known it.

McGurk's army would have to go all the way, all the way to the

White House. Once you began an avalanche, you didn't stop it halfway down the mountain.

McGurk stood up, and began straightening his office before leaving for his other office where important work was done. Soon, he would have to call the United States Attorney General and tell him that the secret police army did not exist.

CHAPTER FIVE

Dr. HAROLD SMITH'S LEMONY face looked unusually acidic.

"Hello, Remo," he said. He sat in the harshly-lit, securely locked depositor's room of the Manhattan Bank with two attaché cases before him. They were open and stacked rim level with packets of new hundred-dollar bills.

Remo looked at the money. Funny how money lost its value when you could have it by picking up a telephone and mumbling a few words, or when there was nothing you really wanted to buy because your life didn't make any difference to anyone but your employer anyway. The hundred dollar bills were what they were. Paper.

"First, let me explain the money. You will establish yourself in New York as a figure in the rackets. We have established that in the eyes of our police targets, a man is identified as a rackets figure, not because he functions in the rackets, but because he has the police on his payroll. In other words, you exist as a racketeer because you pay off police.

"Now, the beauty of this is that you do not have to build — which would take time — an organization of your own. Moreover, it eliminates the risk of your bungling around in loan-sharking, numbers, hijacking, prostitution, drugs and the like which are highly sophisticated."

"You mean the cops will think I'm a gangster if I pay them off and I won't have to mess with the business of being one?"

"Exactly," said Smith.

"And then?"

"Find out the leadership, clean it out, and then we'll dislocate the rest of the organization."

"Why not just let your drones gather evidence and have it appear on some U.S. attorney's desk? I mean, why do the leaders have to be terminated?"

"Because we don't want their organization public. It's our belief that if the organization were made known, in this country today they would not only escape conviction, but could run for public office and win."

"That's bad?" asked Remo angrily. "If they won, we could retire. If they won, we wouldn't be needed. They're doing our job, Smitty."

"No, they're not, Remo," said Dr. Smith softly.

"Don't tell me that some of those people they've been knocking off weren't on your little computer print-outs with some long, complicated plan to get them in trouble with the IRS? Come on, Smitty, who the hell do you think you're talking to? Those guys are doing our job and doing it faster and better, and I think in your aristocratic gut, you're afraid we won't be needed any more."

"Remo," said Smith, his voice tense and low, "your function parallels what these people are doing, so you see them as doing right. But there are differences. One, we use you only in dire emergencies when we have no alternative. Two, we exist precisely to prevent the sort of thing that is going on now. CURE exists so America won't become a police state. We were commissioned so this wouldn't happen."

"That's too subtle for me, Smitty."

"Remo, I'm going to ask you what every commander has asked his troops since he led them from the caves. Trust me. Trust my judgment."

"As opposed to my own."

"Yes."

Remo drummed his fingers on the clean wood tabletop. He had to be careful about hitting things. He wanted to hit. He wanted to smash the table.

"All right. And I'll tell you what every foot soldier has felt since you led us out of the caves: I don't have much choice."

Smith nodded. He gave Remo a verbal rundown on the latest

reports, analyzing the growing police network, the probability that it would be located in the East.

"Our best guess from the number and location of the hits is that they have at least a hundred and fifty men. It would take that kind of manpower pool to be able to move people around into different cities, and take no chances on their faces becoming familiar."

Smith added that a teller had been overly interested in the large amount of cash withdrawn from the bank under one of CURE's cover names and Remo should be careful that he was not the target of a robbery.

"There's almost a million dollars in these two cases. Cash. You'll return what's left at the usual account."

"No," Remo said, eyeing the thin bitter face before him. "I'm going to burn what's left over."

"You destroy American energy when you burn money." There was shock on Smith's face.

"I know, Smitty. You're a real descendant of the Mayflower."

"I fail to see…"

"And I'm just a dumb honkey cop," Remo interrupted, "who, if he knew his folks, would probably see them in blue collars."

"Chiun says you're something more."

"I don't want to be anything more," Remo said. "I'm proud to be a honkey. You know what that is? That's the redneck dirt farmer, not the plantation owner. That's the cowhand, not the rancher. That's the guinea, not the Italian-American. That's the Jewish philanthropist. Me."

"And don't think I don't know how much those people mean to America," said Dr. Smith.

"Those people. Those people."

Remo snatched a packet of bills, fresh and new and packed together as hard as wood. In front of Smith's face, he worked the fibers in his hands, wresting them from each other. The green confetti sprinkled on Smith's lap.

"That was ten thousand dollars, Remo. *Our* ten thousand dollars."

"*Our* ten thousand and *those* people. Our. Those."

"Good day, Remo," said Smith, rising. Remo could feel frustration mounting in the little pillar of integrity. A nice warmth overcame him, especially when Smith tried to say something at the door and could not find words.

"Have a good day, Smitty," laughed Remo. He closed the attaché cases, gave Smith time to get out of the bank, then strolled out into the street to be robbed.

He saw no one who seemed to have any interest in him. So he walked around the block. Still no one. He walked around again, and then saw the same car again, and realized why he had overlooked the targeters. It was a man and woman in the front seat of a parked car. They appeared to be staring lovingly into each other's eyes. Good cover. Of course, *lovingly*, on Remo's third time around the block, was obviously a fraud. The essence of love, as Chiun had said, was its transitory nature. It was like life itself. Short. A brief interlude surrounded by nothing.

Having identified his attackers, Remo walked briskly along Fourteenth Street swinging the two attaché cases. He paused in traffic-snarled Union Square, lest the lovers lose him. He glanced back. No, they were there, in the car following him. There was another car behind theirs. Two tall black men with floppy-brimmed hats jumped out of the second car. The lover and another white man came out of the front car, all moving in his direction. An integrated job. Who said New Yorkers didn't work together in harmony, regardless of race, creed, or color?

Remo decided to circle Union Square to see if they would actually attempt a daylight robbery in a crowd. Far back now, the two cars still stood in the traffic that choked the Square. The four men loped after Remo as he strolled the park. They were packing, but it was not the bulges that gave them away. Armed people walked differently, as if they were surrounding their weapons, not carrying them.

On Remo's second time around the park, the four men split into twos, and took stations on the east and west sides of the small park. Remo headed for the middle. The four men headed for him. The blacks went for his head and each white went for an attaché case.

The cases were not there, however. They were simultaneously cutting up under two black chins with sickening cracks. The whites got the cases in their backs on the way past Remo.

To passers-by, it looked as if one poor man was being overwhelmed by four, and Remo noticed he was the subject of curiosity and nothing more. No screams. No help. Just mild interest. One of the whites fumbled for a revolver and Remo placekicked his teeth to the back of his throat. He imbedded the big floppy hat of a black in the central portion of his brain, and caught the second white with a neat, but not very powerful, elbow thrust. Too strong, and you had to get the suit cleaned. The temple shattered, without releasing blood or brains.

Remo separated the spinal column of the last living member of the foursome with a simple heel chop.

Then came the shock. The curious bystanders were no longer curious. They just continued on their way, stepping over the bodies. The only interruption to the smooth flow was a comment from a woman shopper about the inadequacy of the city's sanitation department.

Remo looked back to where the two cars still sat in traffic. The drivers bolted. The woman dashed toward the East River and the man ran toward the Hudson. Remo didn't feel like running after them, and he walked on with the stream of New Yorkers scurrying toward their destinations, hoping to get there alive.

Remo noticed his shoes were scuffed. At Third Avenue he stopped for a corner shoeshine boy. The boy looked at the tip of Remo's right shoe and took out a greenish, well-used bottle.

"What's that?" Remo asked.

"You can't get blood off leather right with just water," the boy said. "You got to use special solution."

Remo looked down. Indeed. There was a speck of blood. He looked at the bottle. The greenish liquid had caked near the rim from constant use. *New York, New York, what a wonderful town*, Remo hummed.

From a transistor radio in the boy's shoeshine kit, Remo listened to the news. A Mafia chieftain killed in Philadelphia. And the mayor of New York declaring that public insensitivity to social problems was the biggest stumbling block to city progress.

CHAPTER SIX

A HOUSE SUITABLE FOR A New York City racketeer had been purchased for Remo. It was a one-family home, upper middle class Queens. Remo picked up Chiun at the airport along with Chiun's luggage, eight steamer trunks, five large valises and six wooden cartons.

"I was informed we would be moving into a home so I brought a small change of clothes," Chiun had said, insisting that one of the wooden cartons go with them in the cab. Three cabs followed with Chiun's small change of clothes.

The carton, Remo knew, was the television tape machine that had been fitted with a giant cadmium battery in order to tape Chiun's favorite shows while he was en route from Texas. He would not leave Texas knowing that he would miss *As the Planet Revolves* and *Dr. Lawrence Walters, Psychiatrist at Large.*

Remo sat crunched between carton and door in the back of the cab. He gave Chiun a baleful look.

"It is possible that one of the following chariots would get lost and then a moment of beauty would be gone from me forever, a poor shallow moment for a desert of a life," Chiun explained.

"You've been told, Chiun, we can buy copies of the damned shows."

"I have been told many things in my life. What I can touch, I believe," said Chiun, patting the crate that wedged Remo uncomfortably against the side of the cab door. Remo looked over the crate and saw Chiun had even less room proportionately, but was nevertheless sitting comfortably, his body collapsed into an even narrower form.

Then Remo disclosed what was worrying him.

"I picked up a trace when I shouldn't this afternoon in New York City," he said, referring to the blood on his shoe. Chiun did not have to be told about blood or shoe. "Trace" was the signal that a blow was improperly delivered, not so badly that it failed to do its job but badly enough to indicate that precision was going. It was a sign that technique was slipping and any careful artisan took it seriously.

"Anger," Chiun said. "Anger will do that."

"I wasn't angry. I was working four simultaneously. I didn't know them."

"Anger is a poison that spreads throughout a life. You did not have to be angry at that moment. Anger robs your balance. Only dedication and harmony can restore it."

"Yes, I was angry. I am still angry."

"Then be prepared for traces. After traces come accidents. And after accidents, misses. And after misses, comes loss. And for us, loss is…" Chiun did not finish the sentence.

"We will work on harmony, Little Father," Remo said. "But I'm still angry."

The taxi caravan drove down a tree-lined street with neat brick and shingle homes, cars in driveways, children playing on the clean sidewalks. When the cab stopped in front of the house, Remo saw the nameplate already had been placed on the heavy iron gate that guarded the flagstone walk to the house. *Remo Bednick*. So that's who he would be this trip. Remo Bednick.

He supervised the unloading while keeping the attach cases to himself. Chiun's television was turned on immediately and Remo began his harmony exercises, sitting in a full lotus, imagining himself first as matter, then as a spirit, then as a spirit combined with all matter and all spirit. When he eased back into the reality of his surrounding, a neat, furnished home, the anger was still there but it was distant. Like someone else's anger.

He brought the attaché cases downstairs to store the money in the safest hiding place in any house. The refrigerator. When he swung open the door, he saw the space was taken.

Five crimson robes, folded neatly, filled the shelves of the refrigerator. The temperature control was turned to freezing. Chiun was upstairs learning for the 287th time that year that Wayne Hampton's second wife, who had run away with Bruce Cabot, director of Internal Security for Malgar Corporation, was discovering that she really loved her daughter, May Sue Lippincott, and that the two of them might indeed love the same man, Vance Masters, leading authority on heart diseases who was secretly suffering from a disease whose cure he was working on. Dr. Masters did not know he had the disease. He had been about to be informed last September and was still about to be informed as of yesterday.

Chiun could not be torn away from the show; so Remo could not insist Chiun find another place for the crimson robes. It had to be a cool place because the shoddy Korean dye of which Chiun was so proud tended to run.

Remo thought a moment, then remembered the attic. There was a toy chest there. Blue robes filled the toy chest. The basement was hung like a carnival with yellow and orange robes.

Remo took the attaché cases up to Chiun's room. Chiun was in a green robe, entranced that Mary Sue Lippincott was now going to tell Dr. Masters he had contracted the dreaded disease he was trying to cure.

Remo waited silently until a woman appeared on the screen to tell about her exciting new washday discovery. For this discovery, she received love from her husband, affection from her son, the respect and admiration of neighbors, and a general feeling of mental health for herself. All because of new lemon-activated Brah.

Remo unlocked the cases and dumped the money onto the floor around Chiun.

"Keep an eye on this," he said.

"For me?" Chiun asked.

"No. Operating money."

"That is much money," Chiun said. "An emperor's fortune."

"We could take it and run, Chiun. Who'd stop us? This would support your village for ten generations. A hundred generations."

Remo smiled. Chiun shook his head.

"Should I leave with this fortune, I would be robbing the future of Sinanju. I would be robbing my own house of Sinanju, for then our centuries of service would be stained by theft. Generations hence might lose employment because of that."

The village of Sinanju in Korea, as Remo knew, had no crops because of the soil, had poor fishing and no industry, and survived only because for hundreds of years, each Master of Sinanju hired himself out as an assassin or instructor of assassins. The poor of the village lived off the deadly skills of each master.

"A million dollars, Chiun, would last a hundred generations the way you people spend money."

Chiun shook his head again. "We do not know money. We know the martial arts. And should it last a hundred generations, where would the hundred and first find sustenance?"

"You really worry about the future, don't you, Little Father?"

"When one is responsible for it, one worries. Do you now walk blind because of your anger?" Chiun held up a typewritten folded note that had been stuffed into the money.

"Oh," said Remo.

"Oh," said Chiun. "Oh, the note. Oh, the way the man walked. Oh, the weapon. Oh, the blow. Oh, the life. Oh."

Remo read the note as Mary Sue Lippincott returned to the screen. Surprise, surprise, she was going to tell Dr. Masters of his disease.

The note was from Smith. Typed himself, undoubtedly, because of the typographical errors and because it was not the kind of note the director of a research sanitarium would dictate to a secretary.

Notes on Bribery

1. The mark of an amateur is an excessive bribe. Better to come in low than high. When you want something, then raise the offer. Bribery is a bargaining medium.

2. A general weekly pad for a precinct runs $200 to the captain, $75 to lieutenants, $25 to sergeants and $15 to patrolmen.

3. Begin small and upgrade. Let the police's imaginations work.

4. See if you can get to inspectors with $5,000. Lay off the chief and the commissioner because you might get arrested there. If they are taking, it filters up from all the ranks.

5. Buy yourself a Cadillac or a Lincoln from a local dealer and pay in cash. Tip excessively in restaurants. Carry a heavy roll. Good hunting. Destroy the note.

Remo shredded the note in his left hand.

"Destroy the note," he mumbled. "No, I'm going to mail it to the *Daily News* in time for their next edition. Destroy the note."

Remo looked up Cadillac in the yellow pages of the telephone directory, saw it was nearby, walked to the showroom and said to a salesman: "That one."

"Sir?" said the salesman.

"I want that one."

"Now, sir?" said the salesman, rubbing his hands obsequiously. His expensive tie bobbed at his throat. His blondish hair, pasted to his head, glistened under the overhead lights.

"Now," said Remo.

"May I show it to you first?"

"No."

"Well, it lists for eleven thousand five hundred dollars with the air conditioning and the…"

"Put some gas in it and give me the keys."

"The forms…"

"Mail them to me. I want to buy a car. That's all. Just sell me the car. I don't need forms. I don't need a discount. I don't need a demonstration ride. What I need is the keys."

"How did you intend to pay for it, sir?"

"With money, what did you think?"

"I mean financing."

Remo brought the heavy rolls of hundreds out of his pocket. The newness made them snap back almost straight. He began to count off a hundred and fifteen hundred-dollar bills.

The salesman looked at the bills and smiled weakly. He called the manager. The manager looked at the bills. He raised one to the light and felt it. Its newness apparently frightened him. He checked ten more at random.

"What are you, an art lover?" asked Remo.

"No, no. I'm a money lover and this money is good."

"Give me the keys to the car."

"I'll give you my wife," said the manager.

"Just the keys," said Remo. The salesman scurried to the glass enclosed office as Remo gave the manager his name and address for the forms. Ostensibly for the forms. He wanted the manager to spread the word about the man who paid for the car in cash.

The salesman nervously continued his sales pitch while handing Remo the keys to the beige four-door Fleetwood. On his way home, Remo stopped at a furniture store and ordered two color consoles which he did not need, and a bedroom set which he did not need. He gave name and address and paid in cash.

That night, Remo reached the local precinct house and was strangely apprehensive about offering a bribe to a policeman. He had never taken when he was a cop and he knew many who also wouldn't take. Sure, there was Christmastime on a beat but that wasn't taking. And then there were levels of taking. Gambling money, while not good money, wasn't considered dirty by many officers. Dirty money was drug money and killing money. Unless police forces had changed in the last decade, Remo thought there were many who would not touch a cent. For Smith, whose ancestors had made a fortune slaving and then had the gall to lead the abolitionist movement when their wealth was established, to now blandly assume that policemen were tagged with prices like supermarket items was an affront to the very balance of the universe.

Remo got out of the car onto the litter-strewn street and scampered up the worn cement steps of the precinct house. Nostalgia was immediate. Every precinct house smelled the same. Ten years later, a hundred years later. Ten miles away. A hundred miles away. A precinct house smelled tired. It was a combination of the odors of human tension and cigarettes and whatever else it took to make that smell. But tired it was.

Remo went to the desk lieutenant, said he was new in the neighborhood and introduced himself. The lieutenant was formally polite but his face held bored contempt. When Remo offered a hand to shake, the lieutenant took it as if humoring him. In Remo's palm was a folded bill. Remo expected the lieutenant to open it up, look at him and throw it in his face.

He didn't. The hand disappeared smoothly and now there was a pleasant smile on the face.

"I'd like to talk to the precinct captain. Tell him to give me a buzz, will you?" asked Remo.

"Certainly, Mr. Bednick. Welcome to New York."

On his way out, when the lieutenant had a chance to look at the size of the bill, Remo heard him call out, "*Big* welcome to New York City."

And then Remo knew why he had been apprehensive. He had set the bribe up absolutely wrong, hoping it would fail, hoping Smith would be proved wrong. He could have done it right, striking up a conversation with a local patrolman, offering him something for his family, working himself up through the ranks carefully. Instead, he had walked brazenly into the precinct house where, for all anyone knew, he might have been a state investigator, where if the lieutenant had any worries he would exercise them. And it worked anyway. Remo was disappointed.

On the street in the chemical air of New York City, Remo cleared his mind. He was not in the business of failing, and he would not risk it again.

It was fun to drive the big car and play the stereo as if the car and the lifestyle were really his. When he turned into his street, he saw an unmarked police car down the block, visible even in the dark. The unwaxed dullness about it and the small aerial were the giveaway. Anyone could spot them and Remo sometimes wondered why police didn't use real unmarked cars, like red and yellow convertibles and jalopies with flower decals on them. Those would be real unmarked cars, not just a different form of standard police car.

He parked the car quickly and rushed out. What had Chiun done now? It was not uncommon for Chiun to "merely protect himself" or "merely assure his solitude," which, on occasion had called for the nasty and unpleasant disposal of bodies.

Remo bounded to the door and found it unlocked. Inside, a

paunchy man in a business suit sat by a low coffee table in the living room. Chiun sat on the floor listening intently.

"Do not be bothered by the rude interruption," Chiun told the man. "Continue as if we were living in a civilized society."

Chiun turned then to Remo.

"Remo. Sit down and listen to the wonderful stories of this gentleman. How exciting they are. How professional he is. Risking his life every day."

"Well, not now," said the man. "But when I was a patrolman I was in two gun battles."

"Two gun battles," said Chiun with exaggerated awe. "And did you kill anyone?"

"I wounded a gunman."

"Did you hear that, Remo? How exciting. Wounding a gunman and bullets flying and women screaming."

"Well, there were no women screaming," said the man. "Allow me to introduce myself. I'm Captain Milken. Morris Milken. Lieutenant Russell said you wanted to see me. I've been talking with your servant here. Fine fellow. Sort of gets a little bit too excited over talk about violence and things like that. But I assured him that if one house in this precinct is safe, it's this one."

"That's very nice of you," said Remo.

"He said if ever we felt endangered, even endangered by strangers on the block, we could phone him," said Chiun. "For someone of my age and frailness, this is reassurance of most great value."

"We protect our elderly in this precinct," said Captain Milken.

"Yes. I wanted to talk to you about things like that and I'm glad you could come," said Remo. "Chiun, I'd like to be alone with the captain."

"Oh, yes. Of course. I forgot my humble place as your servant and overstepped my bounds. I will return to my place of servitude."

"Knock it off, Chiun. Enough."

"As you order, master. Your word is my command. "Chiun rose and bowed and shuffled humbly from the room.

"One thing about old time dinks. They sure know respect, don't they?" said the captain. "There's a beauty about that old guy's humility."

"Humble as a tidal wave," said Remo.

"What?" said Captain Milken.

"Nothing. Let's talk."

Captain Milken smiled and opened his hand.

"Two hundred a week for you and a proportionate amount to your men. Seventy-five for lieutenants, twenty-five for sergeants and detectives, fifteen for foot patrol. Anything else, we can work out later."

"You've been around," said Milken.

"Well, we all have to live, don't we?"

"This precinct usually doesn't get much business. And there's nothing I can do for you in prostitution and drugs; some other areas have already been taken."

"You're trying to find out what I do, right?"

"Well, yes."

"All right. When you find out, if you say no, I'll stop. If you say yes and think you're not getting enough, then you let me know. But what I do is what I do. I just don't want to be hassled every time somebody swipes a car in this precinct."

"You're paying a stiff price for maybe nothing," said Captain Milken.

"Maybe," Remo said. "It's the way I work."

Milken stood up and took his wallet from his hip pocket. "Anytime you need me, call," he said, opening the wallet and removing a business card.

"That's an interesting badge," Remo said.

Milken looked down at his wallet. Inside its fold was a golden five-pointed star, with a clenched fist in the center. "What's it for?" Remo asked.

"An organization I belong to," Captain Milken said. "The Men of the Shield. Ever hear of it?"

"No. Can't say I have."

Captain Milken smiled. "I think you should. You might find some of our projects personally interesting. Would you like to meet our leader? Inspector William McGurk. A hell of a guy."

"McGurk," said Remo, filing the name. "Sure I would."

"Fine. I'll set it up. I'm sure he'd like to meet you."

CHAPTER SEVEN

JAMES HARDESTY III DESCENDED from the helicopter in a broad rolling stretch of Wyoming where his cattle grazed on the rich grasslands and his ranch hands galloped to the landing zone to meet him.

They called him "Jim" and said among themselves that at heart this multimillionaire was just a cowboy. Hardesty, tall and lean and clean of features, made it to the ground in a short hop and almost pulled the foreman off his horse with the ferocity of his handshake. Jim Hardesty was real people. Jim Hardesty was one of them but for some great passels of money.

If any of the cowboys had spent much time analyzing systems, they would have realized that Jim Hardesty just happened to be real people five times in year A, four times in year B, three times in year C, then back to five times again in the pattern 5-4-3, 5-4-3. He had found this cycle took the least of his time and was sufficient to maintain employee morale.

The shared lunches also worked on a pattern, including buying a round of drinks for the employees he would meet in Cheyenne.

"What other boss as rich as Jim Hardesty would grub down with his hands?" was the question.

"Anyone who understood industrial relations," was the answer from one hand who was given his walking papers the next day.

Jim Hardesty howdied his way through the Bar H ranch, better known to him as V.108.08. The number stood for things like marketability, gross worth, net worth, and a special inventory formula that calculated cattle in relation to the cost of feed.

"You Bar H boys'll be the death of me yet," laughed Big Jim Hardesty.

"Give me some of that good Bar H beef," he said and the ranch hands led him over a hill where a chuck wagon was set up and steaks were being cooked on an open fire.

There was good money in beef, and it was made even better when Jim Hardesty's packing house jacked up the price a notch and Jim Hardesty's trucking line jacked up the price a notch, and Jim Hardesty's city distributors jacked up the price a notch and a half. While violating the antitrust laws in spirit, they did not violate them in fact because Jim Hardesty's friends owned the packing house and truck lines and distributorships, and if they were just figureheads, well, you go ahead and prove it, pardner.

What assured Jim Hardesty's tidy profits was the inability of other people to cut prices on him. He was a reasonable man and in the majority of cases he could show a rancher or a packer or a distributor that when he tried to cut Jim Hardesty's prices he was really only cutting his own throat. And if the man was unable to visualize this, some friends of Jim Hardesty would bring the point home. From ear to ear. It was even hinted darkly in the underworld that you didn't order Hardesty hamburger if you liked 100 per cent beef.

Of course, between Jim Hardesty and the hamburger were several layers of personnel, and Big Jim had been known to use violence only once, when some sidewinders were talking foul in front of ladies. And then it was just fists. Yessir, Big Jim Hardesty was a real man. Salt of the earth.

So when he raised a toast to the "greatest ranch hands a fella could ever count on," the ranch hands were surprised to see him tumble over in a faint. No. He was dead. Heart attack? Wait. Let me smell that liquor. *Pizened.* Who touched the liquor? Get the cook.

The cook tearfully admitted he had poisoned Hardesty when a rope was thrown around his neck. He said he did it to pay off big debts. He pointed to his tattooed arm and showed the needle holes. He was hooked on heroin, he said, and deeply in debt and two men promised to clear his debts and keep him supplied for the rest of his life, if he poisoned Big Jim Hardesty.

"Skin him alive!" cried one of the hands, brandishing a Bowie knife.

"Wait. Let's get the two men. Keep him alive until then."

So they brought the shaking, crying cook to the local sheriff who said he would get a description of the men from the cook and put out an all-points.

The cook saw the two men again that night in his jail cell. They were wearing state trooper uniforms but as always they talked funny, like Easterners. Now, what were they doing in trooper uniforms, these short squat men built like double filing cabinets?

Were they really Wyoming state troopers sent to take him to the penitentiary?

The cook got his answer in a ditch beside a highway. One of the troopers put his pistol to the cook's head and pulled the trigger. The cook didn't even hear the shot. His eardrums were in the next county.

Meanwhile, in Las Vegas, Nicholas Parsoupoulous took a sip of his special wine while rolling in his room-sized bathtub with four of the girls from his chorus line. He was in his late fifties and it was half an hour before the girls realized Mr. Parsoupoulous was dead.

"I thought there was something different," said a blonde. "He seemed nicer, sort of."

At the inquest into his death, it came to light that Parsoupoulous was a key link in a prostitution chain that moved girls from coast to coast. He had been poisoned.

In New York City Police Headquarters, the moon face of Inspector William McGurk was beaming. Wyoming, good. Las Vegas, good.

He walked to the map on his wall. Roundheaded red pins were poked into the map along the East Coast. He picked up two pins now and put one in Wyoming and the other in Las Vegas, then went back to his desk to look at the map.

It was their first venture outside the East, and it had gone like a charm. Right now, Hardesty's killers were back on duty in Harrisburg, Pennsylvania. The men who handled Parsoupoulous should be riding in a patrol car someplace in the Bronx. The timing had been perfect; the logistical problem of moving the men to the targets and back on time had been solved easily. Now, nothing could stop the secret police army.

And the best was yet to come.

No one ever solidified a power base just with force. It had to be followed with something. McGurk ruffled through a sheaf of papers before him. There was large type printed on the pages, like headlines. It was a speech and it was what would follow the wave of killings.

The question was who would give the speech. There really wasn't anyone good enough that he knew of. If Duffy had had any common sense and had not been ruined by that Fordham nonsense but had gone instead to St. John's where people weren't that concerned with books — least of all pinko faggy books — Duffy might have done. But Congressman Duffy was dead.

McGurk read the words of the large type to himself.

"You call yourself New Yorkers and you think you live in a city, one of the great cities of the world. But you don't. You don't live in a city, you live in a jungle. You live frightened in your caves and you dare not walk the streets because you fear the animals.

"Well, let me tell you something. These are your streets and this is your city, and I'm going to give it back to you.

"The animals are going into the cages, not you. The animals will fear to walk the streets, not you. The animals will learn that this is a city for people, not beasts.

"Inevitably, some will call me racist. But who suffers the most from crime? The blacks. The honest blacks. The people who work to try to give their children everything that everybody else wants to give their children. You know who I'm talking about. The good blacks who are called Uncle Toms because they don't want to live in a jungle.

"Well, I speak for them too, and I know they too reject the charge of racism. If I say the littlest child should be able to walk this city without being mugged, is that racist? If I don't want my child or your child raped at recess, is that racist? If I get tired of being gouged to support people who will not work and who threaten me in the bargain, is that racist?

"I say no. And good people…white and black…join me in voicing a resounding 'No,' and sending forth that word now as our program and our platform.

"We say no to the animals. We say no to the thugs. We say no to the vicious and the depraved who prowl our streets. And we will keep saying no to them, until they are removed from our midst."

Inspector William McGurk heard the words in his mind, heard them with such sincerity and force, that he realized only one man could deliver them properly. Mayor William McGurk of New York City. Show 'em a city can work. And then show 'em a state can work. Then show 'em a country can work. And if it could work for a country…

McGurk switched on his intercom.

"Yes, Inspector," came a woman's voice.

"Get me a globe for the office, will you, please?" he said.

"Yes, Inspector. There's a gentleman here with Captain Milken to see you."

"Oh, yes, that one. Send them in."

CHAPTER EIGHT

WHAT WAS REMO BEDNICK'S business?

The question was asked by the moon-faced man, Inspector McGurk. Captain Milken seemed extraordinarily solicitous of the inspector. It was beyond the normal respect a captain shows a superior. Remo filed that away very quickly.

"Business," said Remo,

"What business?"

"Captain Milken hasn't told you?"

"Only what you told him."

"I don't see why I should tell you any more."

"Because I'll take your head off, punk," said Inspector McGurk.

Remo shrugged.

"What can I say? You want me to leave the city, I'll leave the city. You want me to close my businesses, well, then, you've got to find them and do it yourself. You want to be reasonable, I wash your hands and you wash mine; that's something else. That's cash on the barrelhead."

The eyes in the moon face narrowed as McGurk thought of squads of killer cops crisscrossing the country on commercial airlines, registering into motels, eating and drinking, piling up bills.

"He's really okay," said Captain Milken nervously.

McGurk looked at the captain disdainfully. Yes, Remo Bednick was okay, but the captain didn't really understand the reason why.

"Since I don't know what you want," McGurk said, "I'm letting my imagination run wild. The worst. Five thousand a week for what we don't know."

The inspector had batted the ball to Remo's side of the court. Smith's instructions were to bargain, to really play a solid game, and maybe just return the ball. Another racketeer in business. But the instinct that perpetually said slam it into the corner with heavy topspin, was operating even before Remo remembered his instructions.

"I wouldn't give you $5,000 a week," Remo said, watching the moon face. "Make it $10,000. That's what I have on me." The moon face flushed red. Remo disgorged two fat packets of new bills from his pockets and dropped them on the inspector's desk like so much orange rind. The captain cleared his throat.

"There isn't that much extra in this city that isn't tied down by someone else," said McGurk.

"Again, that's my worry."

"Good to meet you, Mr. Bednick." McGurk offered a big, flat muscled hand and Remo took it weakly. He could feel McGurk trying to bruise bone, so he collapsed his hand and smiled. McGurk pressed harder, his facial muscles tightening. Remo smiled. Then he unpopped his hand, breaking the grip like an exploding cellophane wrapper.

"You're out of shape there, sweetie," Remo said.

"You some kind of weightlifter?"

"The weight of the world, Inspector, the weight of the world."

"When we was coming over here, Mr. Bednick said maybe he'd like to meet the commissioner. I told him it wasn't necessary," said Captain Milken.

"Yeah," said McGurk thoughtfully. "Introduce him to the commissioner. Let the commissioner see some of the people we have to deal with. And Bednick, you shake hands with the commissioner. His stays limp."

McGurk shoveled the two packets of cash into his top drawer. Remo left with the captain, who confided with a bit of tension in his voice: "Hell of a regular guy, McGurk."

"You hate him," said Remo. "Why do you say you like him?"

"No, I like him, I like him. Why do you say I don't? I mean I never said I didn't. I really like him."

In the hallway leaving McGurk's office, Captain Milken and Remo passed a gentle-faced blonde girl with skin like porcelain and sky-blue eyes, who turned into McGurk's office, her eyes straight ahead, her lips tension tight.

"Janet O'Toole," whispered Milken when she had passed. "The commissioner's daughter. Sad story. She was raped when she was seventeen. A gang of blacks. Half the department cheered because O'Toole is a real bleeding heart liberal. They'd leave notes around his office saying they found the guys who did it, but they didn't have a warrant and they let them go. One note said they spotted the guys in the act but by the time they finished reading them their constitutional rights, the suspects had all finished and fled. Nasty stuff, you know what I mean?"

"How'd the girl take it?" Remo asked.

"A shame. It wrecked her. The whole thing. She's so afraid of men, she can't look at them."

"She's beautiful," Remo said, thinking of the doll-like features.

"Yeah. And frigid."

"What does she do around here?"

"She's a computer analyst. She works with McGurk on manpower deployment."

"Wait here a minute," Remo said. He turned and walked back into McGurk's office. Janet O'Toole stood with her back to him, looking over a pile of papers on a desk. She wore a long, paisley peasant skirt, neurotically modest, but incongruously, a low-cut white peasant blouse that dipped down off her shoulders and displayed her throat and neck.

"Miss?" Remo said.

The girl wheeled, her eyes startled.

Remo met her eyes for only a split second, then lowered his to the floor. "I...er, I think you dropped this in the hallway," he said, extending his hand with a silver fountain pen he had taken, from Milken's pocket.

He kept looking down. He heard the girl say, in a soft, tremulous voice, "No, that's not mine."

He looked up, making his eyes appear frightened, met her eyes

55

briefly, then looked down at the floor again. "I'm...I'm sorry, but I thought...I mean, I'm really sorry for bothering you, Miss, but I thought..."

Remo spun around and walked quickly from the office. So much for now.

Milken was waiting twenty-five feet down the hallway for him, and Remo gave him his pen back.

"You dropped this."

"Oh, yeah, thanks. Listen, by the way, O'Toole's not in on any of this."

"Any of what?" Remo asked as they resumed walking.

Milken rubbed his fingers together indicating money.

Remo nodded.

Commissioner O'Toole had a head shaped like an egg if an egg could be weak. He looked like Tweety the Canary, but with sadder eyes. When he was informed by Captain Milken that Remo was thinking of entering politics as a businessman, he gave him his theories on law enforcement.

These theories encompassed constitutional rights for suspects, police community relations, greater awareness on the part of a police force for the community it served, and more responsiveness to the hopes and aspirations of minorities.

"How about improving the odds on staying alive?" asked Remo.

"Well, our officers are instructed to use their weapons only in the most dire emergencies and to account for every act of police violence committed."

"No," said Remo, "I'm not talking about the odds for muggers. I mean for people who have committed the great crime of going out at night. What are the odds? Have you improved those?"

"Well, we're living in troubled times. If we increase the responsiveness..."

"Just a minute," interrupted Remo. "Thirty years ago, was your department responsive?"

"Well, no. Not at all. They had yet to be enlightened by the new techniques that..."

"Yeah, well maybe all those unenlightened cops had something to do with people being safer."

"Sir," the commissioner said huffily. "We can't go back to yesterday."

"Not if you don't try."

"I wouldn't want to. That's reactionary."

"Attaboy, label it and put it away. You've got a frightened city out there and if you think another human relations course is going to stop one holdup, then you've got smoke coming out of your ass."

The commissioner turned, signifying that the interview was over, and Captain Milken nervously led Remo Bednick from the office. No racketeer had ever talked to a commissioner like that. He couldn't wait until Bednick had left headquarters, before running to tell McGurk about the confrontation.

But McGurk seemed curiously disinterested, and showed no more curiosity than if Milken had been talking about the dead.

CHAPTER NINE

DR. HAROLD W. SMITH STARED out the one-way glass window of his office in Folcroft Sanitarium. The Long Island Sound was out there. It had risen suddenly as tides will do. No matter how much he expected the tide to rise, its sudden engulfing height always surprised him a little.

Time and tide wait for no man. And neither did CURE or a nation's problems. Smith did not wish to turn around, to have to look at that map again, the big map on the screen across the office.

It was a map of a place he loved very much, but now it was like looking at his mother in the hospital. He had loved his mother very much too, but when she was riven by cancer he could not look at her and he secretly wished that she would die so she wouldn't be in pain any more and he could remember her as a beautiful woman. But that was when he was a boy, and now he was a man who remembered his mother in her hospital bed, frail and desiccated but still his mother.

He spun in his chair and looked at the map of the United States.

Red nodules dotted the East Coast. Each represented an identifiable killing from this organization that had mushroomed like a cancer. And now two solitary lumps had appeared in the western part of the country. And suddenly, time had become critical.

The thing was growing geometrically now. The next jump might be an army, and with that army there would be the first real threat of a police state — particularly if the army decided to seek a political arm.

Smith smiled wanly to himself. How many of those men had enlisted in the secret police army to shape America into some personal fantasy of purity? Why didn't they understand that a police state was the most corrupt of all forms of government?

Smith looked carefully at the map. At a distance, it seemed that the pattern of dots emanated from a central point in New York City. Well, he had committed his reserves there. Remo Williams, the Destroyer, was on the mission. That is, if he was on the mission...if he had gotten over his silly reluctance to go against policemen.

Smith spun back toward the Sound and looked at his watch. Time for Remo to call. He waited five more minutes, and the phone beeped once, lightly.

"Smith here."

"Remo."

"Anything?"

"I think I lucked out. You ever hear of the Men of the Shield?"

"No."

"It's some kind of police organization," Remo said. "I think it might be the framework of what we're looking for."

"Any names?"

"The head of it is an inspector named McGurk."

"Have you contacted him?"

"Yes," Remo said. "I've got him on my personal pad. I'm supposed to see him next week with another installment."

"Remo, we don't have that kind of time. Is there any way you can step it up?"

"I can try," Remo said disgustedly. Smith never had any appreciation of a good job, quickly done.

"By the way," Smith said, "you seem to have gotten over your...er, earlier feelings in this matter."

"Sorry, Smitty, I haven't gotten over anything. Right now, I'm out gathering information for you. If the time comes when more than information is necessary, well, we'll cross that bridge when we come to it."

"Call in tomorrow," Smith said, unnecessarily. Remo's answer was a click as he hung up.

Smith replaced the receiver and spun back toward the Sound. It lapped at the shores of the sanitarium. Was it his imagination or was the tide receding? Dr. Smith peered carefully out the window. No, the tide was not coming back from the big rock on the beach. It hadn't reached it yet; the tide was still rising.

CHAPTER TEN

"MAKE HIM AN OFFER HE CANNOT REFUSE."

Don Mario Panza dismissed his *consigliore* with that instruction. He had been generous. He had been polite. He had been respectful. In troubled times like these, with some of his closest business associates dying in so many mysterious ways, he had been more than generous with the stranger who had moved into his territory and was suddenly paying policemen.

Don Mario Panza had been generous to the point of carelessness and he was not a careless man. There was a new person in Queens who paid off an entire precinct. He also purchased cars and furniture with cash. It was an obvious sign that he wished to get rid of money not to be reported to the Internal Revenue Service.

Remo Bednick was obviously in some business that affected Don Mario. But what? The betting was the same. The numbers were the same. The union business the same. The meat business was even better because no one had to pay the contracts to that Wyoming fellow, Hardesty. And for narcotics, in Queens it was not a business. Not really a business. One even helped to keep it to a minimum. So what was this Remo Bednick doing with an entire precinct on his pad?

Don Mario had been respectful. He had sent an emissary suggesting a friendly meeting. Businessmen should talk, no?

And to this Remo Bednick had said, "Not now, fella, I'm busy."

So Don Mario, being a patient and reasonable man, sent another emissary. A *capo*. The *capo* had explained who he was and who Don Mario was and how Don Mario might possibly help him, how in times like these one needed allies.

"I need another dark sock," this Remo Bednick, this .90-caliber *pezzonovante* had said. He had been putting on his shoes. "That's what I need. Another dark sock."

"I would like an autographed picture of Rad Rex, the wonderful actor who plays Professor Wyatt Winston, noted nuclear physicist in *As the Planet Revolves*," the Oriental servant had said.

The *capo* had repeated the request. And later, upon questioning the *capo*, Don Mario explained that these men did not wish socks or pictures but were making light of the *capo*. The *capo*'s face burned with anger, but Don Mario said, "Enough, we cannot afford unnecessary trouble. I will take care of it."

So Don Mario had sent the *consigliore* who would explain that the great Don wished to help if possible. That the great Don did not like to make requests many times over. That the great Don could not allow in his territory an unknown operation. That the Don, in return, was willing to offer extra protection, if necessary. Perhaps their two businesses could blend. The Don paid for what he got. The Don expected as a personal sign of respect at least a meeting. There could be no refusal on this.

The *consigliore* had returned to the well-guarded fortress home of Don Mario Panza. His face was set. With due respect, he relayed the answer to the offer that could not be refused.

"No."

"Was that all this Remo Bednick said?" asked the Don.

"He added, 'Some other time perhaps.'"

"I see."

"And the Oriental servant wanted to know why we hadn't produced an autographed picture of Rad Rex."

"I see. They still make light of us. Well, perhaps it is our fault. We have not shown them we should be respected. This Oriental servant? Is our Mr. Bednick close to him?"

"I imagine, Don Mario. I never saw the servant serve and he interrupts incessantly without fear of Mr. Bednick."

"So he is not a servant."

"I would think not, Don Mario."

"Is he old?"

"Very."

"How big?"

"If he weighs ninety pounds, he has filled his pockets with lead."

"I see. Well, I have a plan to show Mr. Bednick our force and our power, to show that we could kill him if we wish and that we will stop at nothing to gain our ends. Then he will gladly come — shaking."

The *consigliore* nodded and when he heard the plan, he was once again astounded by the brilliance of his Don, by his uncanny knowledge of human psychology, his wisdom and foresight.

"Magnificent, Don Mario."

"Carefully thought," said Don Mario.

"Oh, another thing," said the *consigliore*. "They sent this." From his briefcase, he removed a white lotus blossom.

The Don thought about the blossom a moment.

"Did they say anything when they gave you the blossom?"

"It was the old man. He wanted to trade for an autographed picture of…"

"Yes, yes, yes. Enough. I have had enough of them," said the Don in a rare display of anger. So they insisted upon creating greater insult. Don Mario threw the blossom into a wastebasket.

"Get me Rocco. Rocco. And three others. They can come from any of the regimes. Rocco."

The *consigliore* nodded. He would have to approach Rocco himself and even though they were on the same side, it was a moment of terror. The mountainous man was terror personified and one did not approach him lightly.

When Don Mario received Rocco, he stood to receive the formal greeting of his greatest enforcer. Rocco towered high above the Don, his face like a great granite crag, his hands the size of shovels. The width of his chest extended beyond a refrigerator, and his eyes were like the darkness beyond the universe.

"It is with great respect that I receive you, Rocco," said Don Mario.

"It is with great respect that I come, Don Mario."

And then Don Mario explained the play because one should explain everything very clearly to Rocco. There would be three assisting him. One for lookout, one to hold the old man, and one to use the ropes. If Mr. Bednick awoke during the night, he should see Rocco's face and then be put to sleep.

"For just a night, Rocco. Not forever," said Don Mario, nervousness in his voice. "Just for the night. We need him. He holds secrets I need. Do you understand? Just for the night he must sleep. As a personal favor to me, Rocco. Just for the night."

When Rocco was being dismissed, Don Mario added:

"Just for the night, Rocco. That is the purpose."

Then Don Mario retired to his safe bed, surrounded by bodyguards and houses rented to his men and a high brick wall. Safe above the turmoil of his business. There would be no such sleep for Mr. Bednick. He would awake to find his servant bound hand and foot, hanging over the bed. Hopefully alive, but distinctly showing the great Don's power to kill this Remo Bednick if he wished. He would also show that he would not stop at doing it. There was only one problem. Rocco. But Rocco had been warned and he had been very good for the last few years. His temper had run away with him only twice.

So with high prospects for a productive evening, Don Mario had slipped into his bed alone, safe in his fortress. He drifted into the dark, comfortable sleep of a man who has planned well. He slept the night and when he awoke, he felt something strange. His toe was touching something soft and thin, like a flower petal. What was a flower petal doing in his bed? He pushed the toe farther and it felt as if it touched drying mud on the sheets. Further, and there was something cold, like clay. No. Liver. Don Mario pulled off the covers and when he saw what was in the bed with him, he let out a terrified shriek, screaming like an unbridled fearstricken child.

"Aaaahhhhhhh!" The voice floated to the bodyguards outside the door and into the courtyard he had supposed safe from attack. The men came running but Don Mario would not let them enter his room. He ordered them to stay out. They must not see this, this loss of power. For in the bed with a lotus blossom in its mouth was the head of the giant Rocco.

That afternoon, when Rad Rex refused to sign his autograph before the taping, a technician's union struck. Word got back to him that the strike would be settled immediately if he merely autographed a picture.

So, looking at his beautiful face for the hundredth time that day, Rad Rex resigned himself to the vicissitudes of life.

"All right. Who should I make it out to?"

"Chiun," said one of the burly pair of men. "To the wisest, most wonderful, kind-hearted, sensitive gift of man. Undying respect. Rad Rex."

"You've got to be kidding."

"That, word for word, will be on your picture or on your face."

"Could you give it to me again?" said Rad Rex.

"Yeah. Chiun. To the wisest, most wonderful...you got that, most wonderful...kind-hearted, sensitive gift of man. Undying respect. Rad Rex."

Rad Rex scribbled away and dramatically offered the autographed picture to the barbarian who even smelled bad.

"Uh, oh," said the man. "You gotta add humble."

"You didn't *say* humble."

"Well, we *want* humble."

"Humble Rad Rex or humble Chiun?"

"Chiun. Between kind-hearted and sensitive."

The picture and two-hundred dozen pairs of dark socks were promptly delivered to a one-family home in upper middle class Queens.

When Chiun saw the picture and the words he conveniently forgot he had requested, a small tear came to his old eyes.

"The bigger they are," said Chiun, "the nicer they are."

He later pointed this out to Remo, but Remo was not interested. He was leaving the house to try to get a line on Inspector William McGurk, too preoccupied even to wonder what 4,800 dark socks were doing in his bedroom.

CHAPTER ELEVEN

BUT INSPECTOR WILLIAM MCGURK was not at police headquarters. He was farther uptown, in an old building at Twentieth Street and Second Avenue, which had once been the pistol range for training city police. The building now had a clothing store on the first floor, and at the top of the second floor landing, a heavy double steel door, under a small sign, M.O.T.S., blocked the way to the old gymnasium and pistol range.

Inside, the range reeked of gunpowder despite air conditioning designed to suck off the smoke and fumes. That was not the only change from the old days, nor was the heavy soundproofing asbestos sheeting that covered the walls. The major change was that instead of lanes, each with a target, there was only one target at the end of the building. And instead of pistols held at arm's length in standard police pose, there were machine guns.

"All right. Let's try it again. Let's get some concentrated fire on that. I don't want to see you spraying. I don't want to see you holding up. I want short bursts and I want that thing riddled. Riddled," yelled McGurk. He pointed to the man-sized dark target.

"Now, you're not going to fire when I count three. You're not going to fire when you feel like it. You're going to fire when you hear this little gadget go click." McGurk held up a child's metal clicker shaped like a frog. McGurk shook the frog. He was in gray slacks and blue shirt and perspiration dripped from his forehead, but there was a grin on his face. Here was a machine that could do what it was supposed to do, it seemed to say.

"All right. On the click," yelled McGurk. The three officers bunched in a semi-circle, readied to fire down the alley at the single target. Nothing. Three seconds. Ten seconds. Twelve seconds. Nothing.

McGurk held up the clicker but made no sound. He watched the men. Thirty seconds. Forty-five seconds. One of the men dried his trigger finger. Another licked his lips and looked over at McGurk. One minute. A minute, ten seconds. The third gunner lowered his weapon.

Two minutes. All the guns lowered. Eyes fixed on McGurk who appeared to notice nothing unusual.

"Hey, when you going to click that thing?" yelled one of the gunners.

"What?" said McGurk, leaning forward as if he had not understood the question.

"I said, when you going...?"

"Click," went the little frog and one man got off a wild burst. The other two machine gunners opened up hesitantly, firing wide of the target.

"Awright, awright," shouted McGurk. "Cease firing. Cease firing."

The gunfire died with a last single shot that plunked a neat hole in the dark outline of a man at the end of the range.

McGurk shook his head and trudged to the alley, standing before the guns, between the men and the targets.

"You three are going to be commanders," he said, still shaking his head. "As we get more men, you're going to be the ones who are supposed to be doing the teaching. You're the leaders and you stink, sewer deep, cesspool wide. Stink. Stupid. Stink."

His face reddened.

"You don't know what I'm talking about, do you. Unfair, right? I didn't play by the rules you learned, did I?"

"Sir," said one of the three men. "You took an awful long time on the click and we relaxed and..."

"Oh," said McGurk, interrupting the man, "I took an awful long time. They didn't teach you that way in police academy training. And since you weren't taught that way, you're not going to learn any other way. Well, how many of you have ever set an ambush? Raise your hands."

One hand went up.

"What ambush?" McGurk said.

"It was these bootleggers…"

"How many'd you kill?"

The man paused. "We wounded three."

"You ever set an ambush where you got 'em all? I mean the way we get them? Well, that's what we're talking about now. You've got to stop thinking like cops, with a 30,000 man department behind you. You're not cops now."

"But we wanted to be better cops is why we joined," said another man.

"Forget it," McGurk snarled. "You're being trained for the ambush. And as we go on and things get stickier, I suggest you get it down pat, because if you don't there may not be enough left of you for a mortician to patch up." They were still unhappy, but their anger was slowly changing to respect.

McGurk sensed this. Standing in front of them, he clicked the frog. The hands went to the triggers and one machine gun almost fired. McGurk laughed loudly, and his laughter helped relax the men. Good.

He walked out of the line of fire and before he reached his observation post clicked again. This time the firing range exploded, with a continuous roar of lead through the air.

"Beautiful," McGurk yelled without turning around. "Beautiful —"

"How can you tell?" asked one of the men.

"On an ambush, you listen for the timing. You don't look," said McGurk happily. "You sounded beautiful —"

The sound of the firing and McGurk's lesson was not beautiful to another man who was listening. The deputy chief had missed McGurk at headquarters and had come here to get him to sign some papers on manpower shifts in Brooklyn. He had been standing outside in the little hallway leading into the range and gym, and had recognized both the voice of McGurk and the machine gun fire. It was definitely a non-standard approach. He knew instantly that in the New York City police force a movement had been started like that in South America. He was a wise man as well as cunning, and he waited quietly, until he had heard enough, and then walked away with his papers still unsigned.

The deputy chief knew there was only one man in the entire department whom he could trust with this information. He was the only man obsessed enough with civil liberties to anger the entire force — the commissioner. The deputy chief had forcefully disagreed with Commissioner O'Toole many times. Once he had threatened to resign and O'Toole had said:

"Bear with me. If we survive the turmoil of the times with our constitutional liberties intact, it will be because men like you stood firm. We're taking the hard road. Please. Trust me —"

"O'Toole, I think you're wrong. I think what happened to your daughter should have showed you you were wrong. But I'll stick, O'Toole. Mainly because in St. Cecilia's they taught me respect for authority. I'm offering this one up to the Virgin Mary because it isn't worth anything to anyone else. Mark it. This is an act of faith in God, not in your competence, Commissioner."

And the deputy chief had followed, enduring the little everyday revolts of a department harassed by militants, abused by the press, condemned by citizens for lack of protection, and called "pigs" by those who never saw a bar of soap. The deputy chief had stuck even when his relatives condemned him for sticking. And he knew that if he suffered, O'Toole must have suffered ten...a hundred times worse. So if there was one person the deputy chief knew he could trust it was Police Commissioner O'Toole. He went directly from the old police range to O'Toole's home, a big brick home in an urban-renewed Irish neighborhood.

They talked for four hours, O'Toole's bulblike face becoming grimmer. During the conversation, O'Toole had to phone headquarters for his nightly midnight check.

Off the phone, he said, "I can hardly believe it. I can't. I know McGurk. Reactionary, yes. A murderer, no."

The deputy chief detailed exactly what he heard.

"Is it possible that you misunderstood?"

"No."

"Is it possible the firing hurt your ears?"

"No."

"Is it possible McGurk was playing some kind of game with recruits?"

"No, dammit. These weren't recruits. These were veteran cops."

"Oh, my Lord. My Lord, my Lord," O'Toole buried his head in his hands. "So it has come to this. Well, go home and tell no one. Promise me that. You'll tell no one. Tomorrow, we'll make plans. I guess we'll have to go to the state…"

"What about the FBI?"

"Maybe they're in it?"

"I doubt it," the deputy chief said. "If we've got one agency we can trust, it's the FBI. The best in the world…"

"Well, yes. But don't phone them now. Come to my office in the morning, and we'll meet them together…"

"Very good, sir…"

The deputy chief did not give it a second thought in the morning. He did not give it a first thought. Outside his own home in Staten Island, he heard the click of a cricket. Or was it a child's clicker? He had no time to think about that either. He went up in a burst of crossing slugs like a body with simultaneous bombs in his bloodstream. The firing lifted him off his feet and sustained him in air for almost a half-second. It seemed like a small eternity to the men firing.

"See what I mean?" said McGurk to his men later. "Beautiful. It works beautifully when it's organized…"

Later in the morning, McGurk locked his office door at headquarters and dialed a special number.

"It's okay now, sir," he said. The response was not pleasant.

"Well, look, sir, I'm sorry," said McGurk. "It was the first time. Sure the outside doors should have been locked. He never should have gotten in. It won't happen again. Yes, sir, I know it was an imposition on you. Yes, sir. I know, sir. Well, I guarantee we won't be overheard again and you won't have to entertain anyone like him again in your home. I'm sorry if he disturbed Janet, sir. Yes, sir. Yes, Commissioner. We won't make any mistakes any more…"

CHAPTER TWELVE

Dᴜʀɪɴɢ ᴛʜᴇ ɴɪɢʜᴛ, while Remo slept on a bed piled high with 4,800 black socks, the press was reporting another wave of killings. The assassination teams had struck again — and this time the pattern had changed.

The first change came in West Springfield, Mass., where the killers left a clue. It was a small square of blue and white striped material and it was found clutched tightly in the hand of Rogers Gordon.

Gordon was the oldest living member of the planning board for America on Parade, one of the country's biggest commercial fairs, and his rank gave him the privilege of riding the overhead cable car through a ceremonial paper ribbon to open the week-long celebration.

Gordon was supposed to ride alone, but at the last minute he invited into the cable car two men with official badges who had accompanied him up the two flights of stairs to the loading ramp. The car moved away from the platform, sliding smoothly along the overhead cable toward the paper strip stretched across the cable between two utility poles. Several hundred people watched from below. Many of them were radio newsmen broadcasting remotes on the opening of the Exposition.

A cheer went up from the crowd as the golden cable car smashed through the thin paper ribbon. Then, over the cheer, a few faint cracks were heard, and all the eyes looking skyward saw Gordon lean against the edge of the car for a moment, reach out behind him toward the two men, and topple over the side.

He landed atop a radio station trailer, plummeting through its thin plastic roof, coming to rest on a small table at which an announcer, Tracy Cole, sat sipping coffee and broadcasting the morning's events at breakneck speed. Rogers Gordon had four slugs in his chest. Even with those, he might have lived a few moments longer, long enough to have told someone that the two men who had presented themselves at his home that morning were not really federal agents who had uncovered his gun-running business; but the cigar smoke in the tiny broadcasting mobile studio effectively prevented anyone from breathing. Rogers Gordon spoke in death, though. As his hand slowly opened, it offered up to Cole — who didn't miss a beat in his delivery — the tiny blue and white patch of material. Police later announced that Gordon must have ripped it from the shirt of one of his killers, both of whom escaped in the confusion.

The clue was the first change in pattern, the first time in the wave of violence that a clue had been left behind.

Another change was discovered in Newark, where the body of an assistant to the mayor was found in the living room of his home in a residential section along the city's shoreline, a jerrybuilt conglomeration of instant blight.

There were three slugs in his head, one through each eye and one through the mouth, gangland's traditional imprint on the squealer silenced. Staring at the dead body like an unblinking eye was an open wall safe. It had been hidden behind a $2.98 print of a Hieronymus Bosch painting mounted in a $129 gilt frame. It was the only piece of artwork in the entire house except, of course, the bowls of plastic fruit on every table.

The wall safe was empty. The city official's wife had been away visiting relatives, had found the body when she returned home and called the police. When they questioned her, she was hysterical and sobbing, not so much from grief as from relief that she was not home when the killers arrived, because she had no doubt that she would have bought the farm too.

No, she tearfully told the police, there had been nothing of value in the wall safe. Just some old mortgage papers, her husband's military record — a bad conduct discharge — and a pair of bronzed baby booties from their first grandchild.

The police nodded, dutifully wrote down what she said and did not believe a word of it. For it was common knowledge that the assistant to the mayor was the man to deal with for a "license" to run a bookmaking shop in town; that he was the man who personally collected the weekly dues from every bookie in town, and that even though he technically collected the money and passed it on to higher-ups, a certain amount of shrinkage inevitably occurred and that shrinkage had made him a very rich man. There was no doubt that the safe had contained a great deal of money.

"A hundred thou," one detective said.

"Sheeit. Five hundred thou," his partner said as they were walking to the car.

"Sheeit, yourself. Maybe a mill."

That overstated the case somewhat. The safe actually had contained $353,716, mostly in large bills. But it was a robbery — the first time money had been taken in the wave of assassinations.

Money and a clue also figured 3,000 miles away. Floorboards had been pried loose and money stolen from its hiding place under them in a Los Angeles brownstone owned by Atrion Belliphant, a Hollywood director whose films always failed but whose lifestyle was fed and financed by the world's largest system of producing and selling pornographic films, a system based largely upon inducing drug addiction in young girls.

His body had been found by his fifteen-year-old red-haired mistress when she awoke from a heroin-induced sleep. Police knew money had been taken because several cash wrappers were found in the flooring cavity under the loose boards.

And again a clue. In Belliphant's hand was a jade and gold cufflink which he must have ripped from the shirt of the killer who had jammed a battery-operated vibrator into Belliphant's mouth and down into his throat, and then turned it on, letting the movie-man jiggle-strangle to death.

A pocket and a cufflink.

Two hordes of cash.

A new pattern.

At the moment, they sat in a pile on the desk of Inspector William McGurk in a small office off the old police range and gymnasium on Twentieth Street and Second Avenue.

McGurk had just finished counting the money and putting it into a large metal strongbox. He wrapped each pile of money in a piece of waxed cloth and carefully tightened them with rubber bands. From a small white memo pad on his desk, he snatched two pieces of paper and wrote down the amounts in each pile. $353,716. $122,931.

He slid the sheets under the rubber bands of the corresponding packets of money.

From his center desk drawer, he took two envelopes. Into one he put a jade and gold cufflink. Into the other, larger envelope, he put a blue and white striped shirt. It was missing a pocket. He also put into that envelope a purchase receipt from a small men's shop in Troy, Ohio, which specialized in tailor-made clothes. He put the two envelopes on top of the piles of cash in the strongbox, locked the box, and placed it in a small floor safe that stood in the corner, its open door showing the empty interior. He locked the safe, then turned around with a self-satisfied expression and walked around to sit at his desk. He looked up as a knock came at the door. "Come in," he called.

The door pushed open and a big beefy man came in, wearing the dark blue, shadow-striped suit that was, all over the country, a uniform for high-ranking police officers. McGurk smiled when he saw the man.

"Brace," he called, rising from his seat to offer a hand. "Good to see you. When'd you get in?"

"About an hour ago. I met the rest of my team on the plane."

"Did you bring them?"

"No. They're waiting at the hotel."

McGurk waved his visitor to a seat. "When's your plane back?"

"Three a.m. from Kennedy Airport."

"You'll be all done by then," McGurk said with a grin, again opening the center drawer of his desk and pulling out a manila envelope.

In the top right-hand corner was a name, but even though Police Inspector Brace Ransom of the Savannah Police Department strained his eyes; he could not read the small, precise writing of McGurk.

McGurk pulled a sheaf of paper from the envelope, to the top of which was clipped an eight-by-ten glossy photo. "Here's your man," he said, pushing the photo across the desk.

Inspector Ransom picked up the picture and looked at it. It was the face of a short swarthy man who might have been Italian or Greek. The man had a slight scar running alongside his left eye toward the corner of his mouth.

As Ransom scanned the photo, McGurk's gravelly voice began to read from information on one of the sheets of paper.

"Emiliano Cornolli. Forty-seven. A lawyer. Known as Mr. Fix. Mob connections through retainers with a number of union locals. Generally represents Mafia leaders in criminal cases and it is an open, but unproved secret, that he buys acquittals by bribing jurors. Lives in an estate in Sussex County, New Jersey, near the Playboy Club. I've got a map here. He's single and technically lives alone, although there's almost always a broad or two around the place. Grounds guarded by two vicious Dobermans. You'll have to take care of them first. If there are girls there, you'll have to take care of them too."

He looked up. "You can be there in about eighty minutes by car. When you get close, muddy up the license plates so nobody can pin down the car rental."

"We sure he's home?"

"Yeah. He's got the flu. Doctor's orders." McGurk slid the map across the desk to the other policeman who picked it up, looked at it carefully, then folded it and put it in his pocket. He pushed the photo back to McGurk. "I'll remember the face," he said.

"Then we're all set," McGurk said.

The Southern police inspector did not move and McGurk looked at him with a trace of a question on his face.

"Bill?" the Southerner said.

"Yeah?"

"I had a chance to read the paper on the plane. That politician in Newark? Was he one of ours?"

"You know you're not supposed to ask," McGurk said. "That's why we've got everything working so well. Teams from all over. In and out. Nobody knowing what anyone else is doing."

"I know all that, Bill. But that money that was missing? I thought there might be a change in plans. Should we take anything tonight? Search the place? That's the only reason I'm asking."

McGurk walked around the desk, leaning in front of it near Ransom.

"No. Take nothing. Leave nothing. Just in and out." Reading the dissatisfied look on Ransom's face, he said softly, "Look, Brace. Next week, we're going to hold our national kickoff for Men of the Shield. I know you've got questions, but keep them to yourself. You'll get the answers then. Until then, just trust me and don't mention anything to anybody."

"That's good enough for me," Ransom said, standing up. He was bigger than McGurk but lacked the impression of power the New York policeman gave off. "How's Number One holding up?"

McGurk winked. "So far, so good," he said. "But you know how liberals are. They start a lot of things and never follow through. You'll see him next week at the big kickoff."

"Okay," Ransom said.

"Listen," McGurk said, still trying to ease Ransom's feelings. "If you get done in time, stop back and we'll have a drink. How are the men you've got, by the way?"

"Look pretty good. One's a lieutenant from San Antonio. The other one's a sergeant from Miami. They both look solid."

"All our men are solid," McGurk said. "The best in the business. That's what it takes to save a country."

Ransom puffed his chest a little. "I think so too."

And then he was out the door, heading down the stairs to where his rented Plymouth was parked in front. He would pick up his two partners in front of their hotel and then make the drive to the foothills of New Jersey. There, a half-hour stop. Then back to New York. A few drinks with McGurk. The airport, and then home. Sweet and simple. McGurk was some kind of planner, keeping all those things straight in his mind, schedules, rooms, tickets, days off so that men were always available. He really knew what he was doing. A helluva cop, Ransom thought.

How much of the whole thing was McGurk and how much O'Toole? O'Toole was technically the leader of the operation, but Ransom knew that most of the work must be coming from McGurk.

O'Toole was a piece of cheese. He had met him once at a police convention, and all he talked about was minority recruitment. Hah. More niggers on the force. A guy with that kind of idea couldn't do anything right. He was glad it was McGurk's show.

Inspector Brace Ransom of Savannah was so deep in thought driving back to his hotel that he did not notice he was being followed by a hard-faced man in a large beige Fleetwood.

CHAPTER THIRTEEN

REMO WAS DISGUSTED, his professional pride injured.

He had followed McGurk from police headquarters to the old police range on Twentieth Street. He had gone as far as the door under the M.O.T.S. sign and then had hidden when the big Southerner, obviously an upper-rank police officer, had arrived. On a hunch, he had decided to follow the Southerner when he left. And now he had been following the rented car with the three policemen for almost an hour and they had not spotted him. He wondered if they would have if he had been driving a circus wagon, and he wondered if he would ever have been so careless back in the days when he was alive. He doubted it.

He had been changing speeds mechanically, without thinking, occasionally driving without lights, sometimes with high beams, sometimes with low, trying to avoid being spotted, and finally he had decided it was not worth it, not for these amateurs, and now for the last fifteen minutes he had been tailing them along Route 80, planted on their tail like a dungaree patch, secure in the knowledge that they were too confident, too much at ease to spot him. They just kept plowing straight ahead, like farmers down a furrow, and it annoyed him because policemen should always be alert.

He tried not to be annoyed. Chiun had warned him about it. "One who permits annoyance begins to pay attention to that annoyance and not to his business. One who does not mind his business soon finds his shelves empty." Right on, Confucius, but they're still annoying.

Ten minutes later, Remo saw the tail lights of the car swerve to the right onto an exit ramp from the highway. Remo quickly tapped his brake to slow down. There was nothing behind him and he slowed enough to let the policemen's car get out of his line of sight, then turned off his lights and sped onto the ramp. Below he saw the car make a left turn and, still with lights off, he rolled down to the corner to see what direction they took. A hundred yards ahead, the road forked and they took the right tine. Remo flipped on his lights and tramped on the accelerator, following them.

He followed them for five minutes through winding twisting roads that curved uphill and sidehill, near the edges of lakes. Then they pulled off into a small driveway that led to a heavy iron gate, set into a high stone wall. Remo drove by, stopped a hundred yards down the road, and parked against the brush at roadside. As he walked back toward the men, he heard the growling and snapping of dogs.

He stood in the dark under an overhanging tree, only ten feet from the men, and listened as the dogs growled and snarled and barked, just on the other side of the giant iron fence. Then, like a record on an old phonograph whose spring was winding down, the dogs' sounds became softer and less frequent. The growls changed to whines; then the whines to whimpers, and then finally silence.

A Southern voice hissed. "Never did see a dog could resist sirloin steak."

"How long'll they be out?"

"There's enough there to keep them for twelve hours. Don't worry about them. They're out of it."

A dry-as-dust Texas voice said, "Ah just hope they ain't no more dogs." He pronounced it *doags* and Remo wondered why Texans couldn't talk English.

"No more. Just the two of them," the Southerner said. "Now come on. We got things to do."

As Remo watched, the two men boosted the third up alongside the twelve-foot-high stone wall. He dragged his way up to the top of the wall, then hung down by his fingertips and dropped heavily onto the other side. Remo could hear weeds snapping under his feet.

He appeared again on the other side of the gate, fumbled for a few moments with the latches, then pulled the gate open and the other two men went in.

What was good enough for them wasn't good enough for him, Remo decided. He spurned the unlocked gate, and moved in one smooth motion up to the top of the wall. Without stopping or slowing, he did a gymnastic flip to the ground on the other side, and as he hit, retracted his legs, collapsing them against his hips, so there would be no pressure on the ground in case he should hit a twig or a branch.

Absolute silence. Nothing.

Only six feet away, he could see the men moving quietly but quickly through the darkness, along the side of a gravel path roadway leading up to the house. The house was an imitation Swiss chalet, stucco and beams and brick, and looked oddly out of place in the gentle hills of the New Jersey countryside. A light was on behind a large first-floor window that was probably in the living room.

Remo moved through the black night, a few feet away from the men. They spoke in harsh whispers. The biggest one with the deepest Southern accent said "Tex. You go around the back. And be careful. There may be a broad or two around."

"What you all going to do?" the Texan asked.

"We'll go in the front some way."

They were about thirty yards from the house now. Suddenly the light on the first floor went off. Floodlights along the roof overhang of the house staggered on, bathing the yard in bright greenish-white light. A shot rang out. It kicked up gravel alongside the three men and they scattered, heading for the cover of nearby bushes.

Remo watched them scrambling around clumsily and, shaking his head in disgust, he dropped back behind a tree. There were no more shots. He listened.

"Rotten bastard," the Southerner hissed, "the gate must have tripped an alarm."

"We better split," Texas said. "He's probably already called for help."

"We came here to do a job. And we're going to do it. This shyster bastard just got off two cop killers. He deserves something for that."

"Yeah, but he don't deserve no piece of my hide."

"He won't get none. Now, here's what we do," the Southerner said.

Remo had heard enough. He moved off to the left, through trees and bushes, silently and swiftly aiming for the back of the house. The rear of the house was dark, but Remo saw a small glint of light near a window, like a flash of metal inside. The woman they had mentioned. She must be waiting inside with a gun.

Remo backed off toward the side of the house, and then charged the wall. On the run, his fingers and toes bit into the rough-hewn exterior stone, and with his legs, he pushed back, then up, until his body had turned from his own momentum, and his legs were moving through an open second-floor window. He was in a small spare bedroom. Before he moved out into the house, he glanced back through the window. The two men were still pinned down in bushes alongside the roadway. He saw their shadows. The third man was missing. That would be Texas, on his way to the house.

Remo moved softly across the carpeted floor, out into the hallway. He heard nothing, and blinked rapidly, forcing blood brainward, willing his eyes to open wider, until finally he could see the interior of the house almost as if the lights were on.

Remo was on a balcony, overlooking the first floor, which was all just one giant room. Down at the front window, sitting on the floor behind a heavy drape, was a short man, wearing a tufted brocade smoking jacket. He held a pistol in his hand.

Remo leaned over the wooden balcony and looked toward the back of the first floor. Yes, there was a girl there. Standing up, which was a mistake, alongside the drapes, which was another mistake, holding a pistol in front of her so it could glint outside, which was another mistake. She was tall and young and brunette and naked, and her nakedness at least was no mistake.

Remo thought of the cops outside, who wanted to kill these two people. They shouldn't do that. But on the other hand, this lawyer had just gotten two cop-killers freed and he shouldn't have done *that*. Six of one, half-dozen of the other. It didn't take Remo long to decide. He had been assigned to jobs like it himself, in the past. If it had been right then, why wasn't it right now? He compromised with himself. He would halve the difference; they couldn't have the girl.

Remo went over the balcony, down the twelve feet to the floor of the room, hitting noiselessly on the flagstone surface. He rolled off to the side, angry because his leather heel had touched with a slight click.

"Did you hear anything?" the man at the front window hissed. He had an oily whine of a voice. Remo saw him turn toward the girl.

"No," she said. "When are your friends going to get here? I don't like this at all."

"Shut up, bitch, and keep an eye on that window and if you see anybody, shoot. Only a few minutes more."

The man was first. Remo moved erect through the darkness of the room. Through the slit in the drapes, he could see the outside yard, brightly illuminated. The two cops were probably still pinned down, maybe waiting for the Texan to charge the rear. Remo hoped he'd take his time. One Alamo was enough.

Then Remo was standing behind the lawyer. He looked down at him, and put out a hand, quietly, and grabbed a splice of nerves in the neck between his thumb and index finger. Without a movement toward Remo, without a sound, the lawyer crumpled forward. Remo held on until the weight of the lawyer's body was heavy against his two fingers, then softly deposited him on the floor. The hell with it. If the cops wanted him, let the cops do it. Remo wasn't about to do their work for them.

And then the girl.

"Emil," she called softly. "I still don't see anybody."

"Emil's not with us any more," Remo said softly. The girl turned, startled, trying to move the gun around to keep it in front of her body. Remo covered her gun hand with his, stopping the hammer from dropping and took the gun away.

She opened her mouth to scream, and he covered her face with his other hand.

"If you want to live, be quiet," he said.

He dropped the gun into his jacket pocket, then put her to sleep. He held her tight against him in an upright position, challenged his mind to remember the last time he'd had a woman, could not, and realized that this girl was nothing more to him than a one-hundred-and-ten-pound side of beef. Chiun would have been delighted.

Remo glanced through the drape and caught a glint of light against a bush at the left rear corner of the house. That would be Texas with his gun drawn. He would be making his move any moment now against the left rear door, leading to a small kitchen area.

Remo carried the girl, straight up like a store mannequin, to the right corner of the house, where a large window overlooked the grounds behind the house. A hundred yards away was a picket line of trees, then heavy woods. Softly, he opened the window and then waited.

"Aiiiiyeee," came the sound. Well, was that stupid or what? The silly-ass shitkicker was coming on with a rebel yell, Remo debated in his mind for a moment whether he should go over and smack Tex around for being silly. He decided not to.

To hell with it. Stupidity was its own reward. Texas would get his someday, all on his own, not because of any cruel god or quirk of fate, but simply because he would have deeply, fully, and richly deserved it.

Then the Texan was trying to pound and shoot his way through the locked side door. He was still yelling like an uprooted banshee. The door resounded with the thumps of his shoulder and fist against it. The pistol shots clicked and whistled off the metal of the door lock.

Remo sighed. Why did cops always think you could shoot off a door lock? It didn't work that way. And this silly bastard would probably stand there all night, yelling and shooting and thumping, unless something was done.

"Balls," Remo said. He propped the girl up over a small table, and moved back through the darkness toward the door that still had not yielded to the policeman's assault. Have to hurry. The other two nit-nats would probably be moving for the front door.

He waited behind the door for another unsuccessful thump as Texas' shoulder slammed against Georgia pine, then reached down and turned the lock. It would open now when the handle was turned. Eventually, even Jim Bowie would have to give the handle a try.

Remo returned to the girl, slid open the window and moved up onto the sill. A moment later, he heard the door give. At almost the same time the front door gave way, and the downstairs was flooded with light from the searchlighted front yard.

In came the police and out went Remo, onto the ground. He hurriedly pulled the girl's unconscious body after him.

He carried the girl to the bank of trees and gently placed her down behind a tree, then tapped her alongside the temple to make sure she would stay out. With luck, she'd wake up after the three policemen had gone; she would get her clothes, leave, and that would be that.

Remo returned to the house. As he got to the back wall, the inside lights clicked on.

"Whoooeee," he heard the Texan yelp. "The sonofabitch done fainted on us."

"That's right. He's just out," came the authoritative Southern voice. "Let's finish him off and get out of here. You didn't see any woman?"

"No," Texas answered. "Weren't no one else in here. If there was, they'd a plunked me coming in the door."

Remo headed for the main gate. As he reached the wall, he heard a muffled shot behind him. So much for one dishonest lawyer. Then he was through the gate and running along the roadway back to his parked Cadillac, disgusted with the three policemen behind him.

They just didn't make cops like they used to.

CHAPTER FOURTEEN

REMO SLIPPED INTO THE BUILDING on Twentieth Street and took the stairs three at a time. He hadn't really pressed it driving back and if the three policemen were coming back, he had only a few minutes lead time.

At the top of the second floor landing was a large metal double door, under the sign M.O.T.S. That would be Men of the Shield, the badge Captain Milken had displayed at his home.

Remo pressed an ear to the door and heard nothing. He tried the handle. It was unlocked. Quickly, he slipped inside and pulled the door shut behind him. He was in a small foyer, still separated from the main room by wired glass fire doors.

There was still no sound, but now he saw a sliver of light from an almost closed door across the room from him. Remo moved inside and found himself in a big open room that he recognized as a onetime gymnasium. Anchors for ropes were still mounted high up on the walls, and there were cleats in the floor where heavy gymnastic equipment had been bolted. At the far end of the room, he saw the vague outline of what at first appeared to be a man; then he saw it was a firing dummy.

Remo crossed the room and peered through the slightly open door. A phone rang.

Two rings and then a girl's voice said, "Hello, M.O.T.S." It was

Commissioner O'Toole's daughter. Remo recognized the soft, almost hesitant tones of her voice.

"No," she said, "Inspector McGurk isn't here right at this moment. He's gone for coffee but should be back any moment. Can I have him call you?"

"Thank you," she said after a pause. "I'll tell him."

Remo peered around the door. The girl sat at the side of the room at a desk, a large accordion-folded computer printout in front of her. She looked down the list, occasionally jotting down a few words on a yellow pad. On the other side of the room, there was another office. The door was open, and enough light from Janet O'Toole's office seeped into the room to illuminate a nameplate on the desk:

"William McGurk."

Remo's ears picked up the sound of voices outside the door to the hallway. Someone was coming in. At that moment, Janet O'Toole rose and went to a filing cabinet behind her desk. Her back was to Remo and he slipped into her office, moved noiselessly across the linoleum tile and entered McGurk's office.

Behind him, he could hear McGurk's powerful ho-ho-ho voice booming, echoing through the empty hall. He heard another voice answer, a softer Southern voice. It was the police officer who had led the hunting expedition.

Remo looked quickly around the office. Nowhere to hide. Just a closet. He opened the closet door and a moment later was up on top of the shelf, his legs bent, his neck resting against the wall. He heard the two men enter McGurk's office and then the door close.

"Pretty girl," the Southerner said.

"Yes. O'Toole's daughter. She's a big help to me. Actually, the brains of the operation. Sit down, Brace, and tell me how it went."

It was too warm for coats. They wouldn't be at the closet so Remo relaxed and let his weight down onto the closet shelf and listened as Inspector Ransom of Savannah, Georgia, explained how he had just assassinated a lawyer in New Jersey.

"Funny thing," Ransom said. "He pegged some shots at us and then...hah, he fainted."

"Fainted?"

"Yup. He was out like a light when we finally got into the house. All cuddled over, still holding his gun."

"Did you?"

"We took care of him. But there wasn't anybody else there. No girl or anything."

"Well," McGurk said, "that's just too bad for him. Couldn't even celebrate his own departure with a bang."

The two laughed together in the easy way of policemen who know everybody else in the world is crazy.

"Good job, then," McGurk said. "You be leaving soon?"

"Right away. The men are checking us out of the hotel. I'm going to pick them up and get back to the airport. So...what's next?"

"Well, next week, we're going to publicly announce the formation of the Men of the Shield. A new national police organization."

"Maybe I'm just stupid, Bill, but I don't really understand where we're going."

"Where we're going, Brace, is we're going to make this a national pressure group for policemen...to fight for law and order. My retirement papers should be back in a couple of days and I'll be able to give it full time. You, me, the forty men we got on the inside with us, we're all going to be the nucleus. But before long we're going to get every policeman in the country in it. Can you imagine the power we'll have?"

"Be a helluva lot of votes if you ever decide to run for president," the Southerner said, chuckling.

McGurk paused before answering. "Don't discount it, Brace. I might just do that."

"What about our...er, assignments?" the Southerner asked.

"Well, for the time being we're going to put all that on a shelf. We're going to go public; we're going to start solving crimes in public. Think about it for a minute: we've been getting rid of some bad apples, but we've also been exposing the public to a wave of violence. You've seen the headlines. More killings. Gangs at war. All that crap.

"Well, soon, now, we're going to have every cop in the country with us. Every policeman whose hands are tied by grafting politicians, by spineless brass...all of them pumping information into us. And we're going to start tying up loose ends and we're not going to be afraid to act. We'll start filling the jails. We'll be bigger than the FBI."

"And what if we bomb out?" the Southerner said.

"Then, we'll just have more assignments," McGurk said with a harsh laugh. "But we're not going to bomb out. We're going to start in with a big flurry. We're going to announce a national war on crime, and guess what the first two cases are that we're going to investigate?"

There was no answer, and McGurk answered his own question.

"That smut king out West and that gun-runner from Massachusetts. You asked before, why the clues? That's why the clues. We've got the other half of the set and we'll use them to solve the case. That'll get the Men of the Shield off to a ripping start, and then watch our membership zoom. We're going to be the biggest thing in the country."

"You sure you're not running for president?"

"If I did, would you vote for me?"

"As often as they'd let me."

McGurk chuckled. "With that kind of backing, how could I refuse? Might be nice to have a cop in the White House anyway…just for four years to straighten this country out."

"Amen."

"At any rate," McGurk said, his voice settling back down to business, "next week O'Toole's going to send telegrams to all our members — you'll get one — to get you all off duty and here for the kickoff. I'll be seeing you then."

"Bill, it sounds like we gonna have us some fun."

"Yeah. And we gonna do our country some good," McGurk said, imitating the Southerner's accent.

"Ah never woulda guessed," the Southerner said, parodying himself, "that you was a kinsman. Now, Ah gotta buy you all a drink."

Remo heard the sound of a chair sliding back. They were getting up now, probably to go out. Then the door opened. He heard the girl's voice say something softly.

"What's in the package, Janet?" McGurk boomed.

"A birthday present for my dad. I was going to put it in the closet."

"Fine, fine. I'm going downstairs with my friend here to see him off. I'll be back later. You'll be all right?"

"Yes, Inspector, thank you." Her voice was tiny, almost apologetic.

Remo heard the front door of McGurk's office squeak. He heard heavy footsteps...the two men...moving across the rug toward the door. He heard the girl's softer footsteps moving toward him. The closet door swung open and light splashed into his face. Her hand reached up to the shelf, holding a package wrapped in foil. Across the room, Remo could see McGurk and Ransom just going out the door. Janet O'Toole saw Remo. Her mouth opened to scream. Remo reached down and put his hand around her mouth, sealing off her shout, and then with both hands pulled her up onto the wooden shelf of the closet.

The office door closed.

Remo said, "I'll do anything if you don't tell on me," and then began to sob softly.

CHAPTER FIFTEEN

NO ONE FEARS A WEEPING MAN. So Remo made real tears come and as he did he was able to slowly release his hand from Janet O'Toole's mouth, and she didn't even realize it. Nor, for that matter, did she seem to realize that she was lying next to him on the top shelf of an office closet.

"I'm so ashamed," he said tearfully.

"What are you *doing* here? You're that Mr. Bednick, aren't you?"

"Yes," he said. Remo Bednick. I came to look at you. But they almost caught me while I was peeking and I hid up here so they wouldn't see me and then you caught me and I'm so embarrassed and ashamed."

"But that's so silly, Remo. Why did you want to see me?"

Careful now, Remo, not too fast. "I don't know," he said. I just wanted to."

"Well, why didn't you just come in the front door and say hello?"

"I was afraid you'd laugh at me," Remo sniffled.

You are the rotten bastard to end all rotten bastards, Remo told himself. Chiun was right, you lack character. He ignored the tiny voice of self-rebuke. He noticed Janet was wearing another low-cut blouse and lying down, her head on his arm, the fullness of her breasts blossomed against the elastic of the blouse.

"Why should I laugh at you?" she asked.

"I don't know. Girls always do. Because I'm shy I guess, and I'm afraid of women."

"When you were in my office that day, Inspector McGurk came out, and he sort of hinted that you weren't afraid of anything."

"But that's men. I'm not afraid of men. Only women. Ever since I was a little boy." Her body touched his along its full length. The shelf of the closet was damned uncomfortable, but he did not want to move, did not want to remind her they were in the top of a closet. If he had to cure her, he'd do it here. Anything for mental health.

He sobbed again. He wished the closet door was closed, shutting out the light; so if he grinned, she would not see his face.

"Oh, you poor thing," she said. "Now, don't cry." She put her left hand up to the side of his face to pat it tenderly.

His left arm was under her neck. He held it there, waiting for her weight to eventually bring her neck down against it. There. She was touching his hand with her neck. His fingers found just the right place. Softly he kneaded the nerves in her neck, under and behind the jawbone, delicately, almost so that she would not feel the touch.

"You mustn't be afraid of women," she said softly. "They won't hurt you."

"I knew *you* wouldn't hurt me," Remo said. "That's why I sneaked up here to see you." His fingers were moving swiftly now on her neck, as if typing tapping typewriter keys.

"No, I would never hurt you, Remo," she said. "Not me. Not you."

She put her face closer to his. He slowed the sobbing. No point in getting ridiculous about it. She continued to pat his face and now she let her fingertips glide down the side of his face from temple to jaw, then back to temple, and did it all over again. The nerves in her neck were working.

"Do you feel better now, Remo?" she asked.

"I'm glad you're so understanding," he said,

"I do understand," she said. "I understand you and your problem too. Oooohhh. I just think you've met the wrong kind of women before. Women who expected you to be something you're not...who wanted you to push them around and demanded more from you than you were able to give." He had reached his right hand over her hip now and was touching the flesh of her back through the thin blouse.

He let her keep talking. "But I'm not that kind of girl," she said. "No man is going to push me around. Not any more."

She paused. Remo said, "I knew you'd understand."

"Understand? Of course, I understand. All you've needed all your life is a little control. Someone to guide you. Ooooohhhh." He was working both her neck and her back now. She moved her body closer to his on the shelf.

"I knew there was something wrong with you when I first saw you," she said. "You blushed and looked away when you spoke to me. I knew then that you needed a little discipline. Ooooooh. Open your belt."

He hoped McGurk would be kept busy downstairs. He removed his right hand from her back and opened his belt buckle.

"I'm tired of men who try to be bossy," she said, her voice no longer soft and pleading. "Women should rule the world."

"I've always known it," he said.

She opened his zipper. He kneaded her neck. "Ooooohhhh," she said. "Woman is the more important of the sexes. We are the ones who call the shots." He returned his hand to the small of her back. "Uuuummmmmm," she said. "Yes, women should be masters, not mistresses. Do you agree? Say you agree."

"I agree," Remo said. "I agree."

Then she was pulling up her long shirt and rolling over on top of Remo. "Even the position," she said. "Even in the position, the woman should be topmost."

"Oh, please don't talk like that," Remo said. "You frighten me."

She was on top of him now and both his hands were free and he worked both sides of her neck.

"I'll talk any way I wish and the sooner you realize it the better," she said sharply. "Do you understand?"

"Yes, I understand." Enough. He gave the nerves in her neck short, brutal final twists, and suddenly, uncontrollably, she was on him, around him, smothering him, her mouth on his, her body swallowing him, her head softly thumping against the ceiling of the closet as she rocked up and down, her feet kicking hats onto the floor. Ooooooohh. Uuuummmmm. Do as I say, not as I do. Up. Up and in. Over and out. No, not over and out. Up and in. More and more. Down with rape and up with humping. Up, up and away. Fly with me. Fly with meeeeeeeeeeeeeeeeeeee."

Then she stopped and lay still, her head on Remo's chest. He heaved his chest a little as if he were still sobbing.

"No tears now," she lectured. "What we've just experienced is normal and healthy. Right? Right. Say it. It's normal and healthy."

"It's normal and healthy," Remo said.

"You'd better believe it," she said. "And it's fucking great too."

"Should I say that too?" Remo asked.

"No, that's all right," she said.

"Good," Remo said. "It's never been like this before," he added truthfully, after trying to remember if he'd ever gotten laid before in a closet.

Oh, yeah, there had been once in a closet, but not on a shelf. A shelf would be a separate category, wouldn't it? I mean, you couldn't just say a closet, and mean any kind of closet or anywhere in a closet. He remembered the other time was a walk-in closet with a couch. Now, that's not even like a closet. More like a room. But a shelf, man, was a shelf. It really belonged in the shelf category, not in the closet category. So this, therefore, was a new experience. Right? Say right, Remo. Right. He was still unconvinced. He would ask Chiun when he went home.

"It may never have been like that before," Janet O'Toole said to Remo, "but it will be like that again if you just do as I say."

"I will. I will."

"All right. Don't forget it. And Remo, I'm really glad that I was able to help you get over your problem."

"So am I."

"But now we have to get out of here before anyone returns."

Remo had been thinking that very thing. They dismounted from the closet, and moments later when McGurk returned from downstairs, Janet was at her desk again and Remo was perched on the edge of it, looking at her lovingly, shyly.

"Bednick," McGurk said. "What are you doing here?"

"I was just passing by," Remo said, standing up and turning to face him. "Thought I'd drop in." He winked at Janet.

"You've got no business here?"

"Nope."

"Then clear out. I have to put up with your kind at headquarters. But I don't have to do it here."

Remo shrugged. "Suit yourself." He leaned over to Janet and McGurk, for the first time, noticed the wrinkled front of her blouse, the slightly tousled look of her ash-blonde hair. "See you?" Remo asked her.

"Don't call me. I'll call you," she said softly, but sternly. "Maybe."

Remo blushed, only for her, then turned and walked quickly past McGurk, out into the hall through the large gym room, and into the hall leading downstairs. McGurk watched him go.

"I don't trust that one," he said to Janet. "There's something animal about him. The way he moves. It's like watching a tiger in a zoo who's just waiting for the zookeeper to open the door and throw in food."

Janet O'Toole giggled. "A tiger?" she said. She giggled again. "More like a pussycat, I'd say." McGurk turned and his eyes met hers. For the first time he could remember, she did not look away.

Smith must have him wired, Remo thought. It seemed every time he walked in the door, two minutes later Smith was on the telephone.

"Well?" came the acerbic voice.

"Well, what?"

"Have you anything to report? There were a number of incidents yesterday, in case you hadn't noticed, and our friend in Washington is worried."

"He's always worried," Remo said. "Don't you be like him."

"Things are very grave," Smith said.

"Even graver now," Remo said. "There was another one tonight."

"And you couldn't stop it?"

"Stop it? I helped. I think it was a great idea. Just imagine. Forty cops, running around this country, putting out the garbage for all of us. Like wow, man. That's New York talk, Smitty."

"Did you say forty policemen?"

"Forty."

"That's impossible," Smith said.

"Not impossible. That's what there are."

"It can't be. There are too many missions, too many different places across the country. How could they do all that with only forty men?" He paused. "Perhaps if they had a computer...working out schedules and travel arrangements et cetera? Maybe. Logistically, it's brilliant." Smith was now very much the bureaucrat, impressed by another bureaucrat who had found a new and better way.

"Like that, huh?" Remo said.

"Give credit where it's due. Even to the enemy," Smith said. "Is McGurk the leader?"

"I'm not sure yet. And don't call him the enemy. I think he's doing a necessary job."

"And I wonder, Remo, if perhaps you're not too close to these men? Maybe you're laying down on the job?"

"Only in closets," Remo said and hung up, angry because Smith had said what Remo had been trying not to think. That he was moving slowly because the cops and he belonged to the same fraternities of heartbreak and frustration.

He looked at the telephone.

"You worry, my son?" Chiun said from his position on the floor in front of the couch.

"It is nothing," Remo said.

"No, it is something," Chiun said. "It is more of your good guys and bad guys. You must cleanse your brain of such nonsense."

"I'll work on it."

"Good."

CHAPTER SIXTEEN

THE RUFFLED BLOUSE OF JANET O'Toole was on McGurk's mind all night. He tossed in bed thinking about it. He had no doubt that Remo Bednick had somehow bedded Janet, right under his nose. She had the happy look of the well-laid, and the blouse was just another link in the chain of evidence.

More than crooked lawyers, more than soft judges, more than Mafia thugs, this outraged McGurk. He had always felt sorry for the girl, ever since he'd learned her sad story. And then, somehow, he knew he had fallen in love with her. Every time he had looked at her he winced inwardly, thinking of that fresh young beauty with so much capacity for love going to waste. But now, wasting that love on Remo Bednick, a mob creep, well, that was outrageous.

But that she had, he had no doubt.

After Remo had left the office, McGurk had demanded of her, "What were you two doing up here?"

The old Janet would have rainbowed through pink and purple and vermilion; she would have stuttered, stammered, looked away and finally run from the room in tears. But this Janet looked at McGurk coolly, met his eyes straight on, and said, "I'd break your heart if I told you."

"Try me," McGurk said.

"Too late. I already tried *him*."

And then she wouldn't talk any more. She dismissed him as if he were a tardy schoolboy and she an angry teacher, and that infuriated him more.

The fury was now full upon him as he lay in bed. The first time he had met Remo Bednick, he had picked out a role for him. Bednick would be one of the men framed for the two killings that the Men of the Shield would solve first — the two murders for which the evidence reposed in McGurk's safe.

But now he put that idea behind him. He made up his mind on what he would do and once he had made up his mind, he put the problem aside and fell immediately asleep. No need to stay awake, to toss or turn. The decision was made: Remo Bednick would die. And McGurk would permit no errors. He would lead this mission himself.

If he had had any second thoughts, they were dispelled the next morning when he arrived at his daytime office in city police headquarters.

With her long skirts and peasant blouses, Janet had become like a piece of furniture. But who was this leaning over the desk, near the computer console? This girl wore a micro-mini of shocking pink, and as she leaned over away from him, the skirt rode up over her hips so that her panties were visible, displaying not only long legs and creamy white thighs, but buttocks clad in pink nylon. When she turned around he saw that she wore a thin pink jersey blouse under which she wore no bra. Her firm young jugs bounced, from no more impetus than her smile, as Janet O'Toole looked at him, and said "Good morning, Bill. Why is your mouth hanging open?"

Remo Bednick would pay for it.

Without a word, McGurk walked past her and into his office and called three men in different city precincts, and told them to meet him after their day tours, at his Men of the Shield office.

Before going to M.O.T.S. in the afternoon, he drove to the house in Queens where Remo Bednick lived. The whole thing would be simple and straightforward, and he looked forward to leading the mission. He told the men he would lead it when they arrived at his office shortly after five.

"When?" one of them asked. He was a tall police sergeant named Kowalchyk. His face was stolid.

"Right now," McGurk said.

"I don't like it," Kowalchyk said. "The whole idea was never do a job in your own city. And here four of us are going out on this one. Why?"

"Because we don't have enough time to wait to get a team in. This guy has found out about us. He can blow the whistle unless we move fast," McGurk lied. He stared blandly at Kowalchyk, eyeballing him until the sergeant looked down at his feet.

"Okay," McGurk said, "any more questions?"

No one answered.

"All right. We'll do it the way we learned at the firing range. Cross fire, on the click. No mistakes. Take a look at this layout I've drawn up," he said, and reached behind him for a piece of paper on which he had sketched the outlines of Remo Bednick's house in Queens.

Chiun had insisted upon cooking duck. Remo hated duck so he sulked. He sat in the living room watching television, trying to drown out Chiun who was singing in the kitchen.

"Duck contains all the nutrients necessary for life. White American fool does not like duck. Is any further proof necessary of its health-giving qualities? White American fool will be dead at sixty-five. Master of Sinanju will live forever. Why? Because he eats duck. White American fool prefers hamburgers. Here I am, world. White American fool. Quick. Stuff me with hamburgers. Give me mono-mono gluto-gluto. Chemicals. Poisons. With mustard and ketchup on a seeded roll. Plastic seeds. I like plastic seeds. I like chemicals. I like poisons. But I hate duck. Oh, how smart is white American. How clever. Master of Sinanju should feel honored to know him."

And so he rattled on, and Remo tuned him out and tuned in Harry Reasoner who was just as funny and not nearly so arrogant.

The news had just gone off and Remo had turned off the television when Chiun appeared in the doorway to the kitchen, his white robe swirling about him.

"Dinner is served, Master," he said.

"Thank you," Remo said. "I believe I'll have some brandy with my duck. A full quart. Something cheap and unobtrusive."

"Oh, yes," Chiun said. "Brandy would be very good. It has many additional poisons that one does not get in hamburgers. May I suggest also that you try motor oil after you finish eating?"

"We won't have any motor oil left," Remo said. "Didn't you use it to cook the duck?"

"You are insolent," Chiun said. "The recipe has been in my family for hundreds of years."

"No wonder all of you have become assassins. The heartburn theory of criminal behavior. That's why the Italians have the Mafia. It's all those peppers they eat."

Chiun jumped up and down like an angry child.

"Your insolence is beyond measure."

"Your duck is beyond description," Remo said, and then, unable to keep a straight face any longer, he laughed out loud.

Chiun's anger faded with the laughter. "Oh, you make sport of the Master of Sinanju. It is wonderful to be so clever."

The doorbell rang. Chiun moved quickly to the front door. "Do not move yourself, oh, good guy-bad guy. Your faithful servant will see who dares intrude upon your world of wit and wisdom."

Chiun moved through the living room, the formal dining room and into a small alcove, and opened the front door. A tall lean man with a stolid face stood there on the first step, looking down at Chiun.

"Remo Bednick?" he asked.

"Do I look like Remo Bednick?"

"Call him. I want to see him."

"May I tell him who is calling?"

"No."

"May I state your business?"

"No."

"Thank you," Chiun said. He closed the door tightly behind him and walked back inside.

Remo was standing near the couch. "Who was it?" he asked.

"No one of consequence," Chiun said. "Come. The duck will get cold."

They sat in the kitchen, digging into the duck, Remo trying to hide his distaste.

Both pretended not to hear the doorbell which brawked incessantly through the meal.

Twenty minutes later, they sipped mineral water.

"Well?" Chiun said.

"The water's great," Remo said.

Braaaawk.

Remo held up his hand. "I'll get the door this time. It might be someone who wants to steal your recipe for duck."

"I see somebody coming," Kowalchyk hissed from the steps. "It don't look like the chink."

"Okay," came a voice from bushes alongside the house. "Everybody be ready."

"Right."

"Right."

Remo opened the door and tried not to laugh. The policeman stood there in plain clothes, his hand near his jacket pocket, slightly turned from Remo, ready to hop down the stairs and begin firing. How clumsy could you get? Remo was beginning to get annoyed with these graceless cops.

"Yeah?"

"Remo Bednick?"

"Yeah."

"Come down here. I've got something to show you."

The cop headed down the stairs. Turning his back on Remo meant that he had help. The bushes. There was someone in the bushes. He listened for a moment. More than one. All right, Remo thought. He moved up close to Kowalchyk, moving with him, in time and in unison, making it impossible for his target to be separated from the policeman's.

At the bottom of the steps, the policeman turned. But Remo was right behind him, and he moved around the policeman, turning him again, and now stood facing his own house, using the cop as a shield between himself and the bushes.

"What is it?" Remo asked.

"Just this," the cop said, pulling his hand from his jacket pocket. The hand had a gun attached. Remo heard a click, like a cricket. He heard pistols cock. The cop in front of him was trying to squeeze the trigger. Remo took the gun from him and cracked him alongside the temple with his elbow. The policeman crumpled and fell, and Remo went for the bushes in a rolling dive. Shots clipped around him.

Chiun was right. Let yourself get annoyed and soon the shelves will be empty. There were police on both sides of him. Both sets of bushes. That's what he got for being careless.

There were two behind the bushes on the left and Remo was on them before they could spin and fire again. They dropped like a jumped-on soufflé as Remo moved into the two of them with knuckles and hands. Three down. One to go or more? Two shots skidded into the bushes near Remo. Then there was silence. He heard the breathing of only one man. Just one.

Remo went up and over the bushes, across the walk and into the bushes on the other side, and slapped the gun away from the man crouched there.

It was McGurk.

He stood up and faced Remo. Slowly, sadly, he looked down toward the gun that lay at his feet.

"Don't try," Remo said. "You'll never make it."

Remo heard a groan behind him. It was the last dying gasp of the policeman on the walk. Remo felt sick.

"These men cops?" he asked.

"They were," McGurk said.

Remo hadn't wanted this assignment. And now three policemen were dead. Three cops who probably thought they were doing America a service by getting rid of Remo Bednick, Mafia thug. No more. Remo would kill no more policemen. Chiun could, if he wished, make fun of good guys and bad guys, but there *were* good guys and bad guys. And cops were among the good guys, and Remo had once been one of them.

So no more.

He looked again at McGurk, who said, "Well?"

"Well, what?"

"Aren't you going to finish me?"

"Not now. Why'd you come after me? I paid up. I didn't get in your way."

"The girl."

"Janet O'Toole?"

"Yeah."

"You mean you got three cops killed because somebody got into her pants?"

"Not just somebody. A mob punk."

"McGurk, you're a bastard," Remo said.

"The colonel's lady and Judy O'Grady, Bednick. We're both in the same racket. We just go different ways."

And then, because it seemed like a good way not to have to kill McGurk, Remo said, "And what if we could both go the same way?"

McGurk paused; he was thinking; then he said carefully, "Like to have you aboard. You've got some talent."

"It's how I make a living."

"I thought you were a gambler," McGurk said.

"No. I'm a hit man. And I pay well just so that I don't get hassled by the bulls every time somebody loses a hubcap."

"Whatever you get, come with us and I'll double it," McGurk said.

"How?" Remo asked. "By selling tickets to the policemen's ball?"

"Don't worry about that, Bednick. We can afford you. We've been planning to get a pro in anyway."

McGurk, a moment ago, had been thinking.

Now, Remo noticed, he was talking rapidly, forcefully. He had something in mind.

"We? Who's *we*?"

McGurk grinned. "Me and my associates."

"Well, you'd better tell me about your associates," Remo said.

And there, behind a bush in Remo's front yard, McGurk told him. About the forty cops around the country who now served as a killer squad, to mete out justice to those for whom the law's justice had been ineffective. And he told him about the Men of the Shield, a national organization of policemen, that was going to fight crime and that could someday be the nation's most powerful lobby.

"Just think of it...nationwide power at the ballot...somebody who could work for law and order for real," he said. A grin cracked his face.

"If you come with us now, Bednick, you'll be safe. If you don't, the Men of the Shield will get you. Sooner or later."

"You the boss?" Remo asked.

"As far as you're concerned." He stood looking at Remo, meeting his eyes straight on. Remo's turn to think. Unless he wanted to kill McGurk, he'd have to go along. And he didn't want to kill any more cops. And how could Smith complain if he infiltrated the organization? Isn't that what he was supposed to do?

"You got a deal, McGurk," Remo said. "But one thing."

"Which is?"

"The girl is mine. You never had a chance with her anyway. You listened to what those long skirts told you, and didn't pay any attention to what those tight blouses said. She's mine."

McGurk shrugged. "She's yours."

He picked up his revolver and slid it back into his holster. Later, leaving the yard, he was glad he had decided not to shoot the punk with the small .25-caliber pistol he had also stashed in his pocket.

McGurk had a better plan now for Remo — one that would solve his problems with the leadership of the Men of the Shield *and* with Janet O'Toole. He would learn no more about the Men of the Shield than would be necessary for him to die.

CHAPTER SEVENTEEN

THE POLICEMAN LUNGED, WAVING the knife before him. Remo stepped aside and brought the heel of his hand, down on the wrist to which the knife was attached. The knife fell onto the wooden platform with a clank.

Remo moved in and grabbed the policeman's hand in his. He pressed the man's fingers into his hand and the man screeched and dropped to his knees in submission.

Remo released him and turned and looked away to the three other policemen sitting on the edge of the stage. He opened his own hand and extended it forward for the men to see. In his palm was a six-inch-long piece of highly polished wood, shaped roughly like a dog's bone.

"This is it," Remo said. "The yawara stick. The quickest way I know to cause pain."

"Why that?" The question came from one of the policemen sitting on the stage. He stood up and repeated it. "Why that? Why not a toe in the balls or a fist in the kidneys? There are a lot of ways to cause pain."

"That's right," Remo said. "There *are* a lot of ways and most of them stink. If you hit the guy too square in the cubes, they'll have to cart him off in an ambulance. Pound his kidney too hard, and he'll be riding a hearse. That's assuming you don't just miss and he doesn't smack the crap out of you. But in close, the yawara stick can't miss. You just grab his hand, squeeze the ball of his thumb up against one of these knobs, and that's it. That's because the nerves of the hands are so sensitive to pain. Pain, but no injury. That's why."

The policeman who was standing shrugged. He was a tall rawboned cop from St. Louis with flaming red hair and a jutting jaw and an absolute absence of humor. He shrugged as if to say "chickenshit bullshit," and then said, "Chickenshit bullshit. It worked 'cause you had him."

"Look, pal. Why don't you just take it on faith? I'm your training officer. That's why McGurk has me here."

"Training officer or no training officer. You keep your funny little piece of wood. I'll settle for a right cross anytime."

"All right," Remo said, walking up close to the man. "Let's see the right cross."

Without warning, the policeman swung, a short hard right hand at Remo's nose. The fist would have gone through wood, but it had no chance to prove it. Remo grabbed the fist in the air with his left hand. He brought his right hand over and pressed one of the bumps on the yawara stick down upon the back of the policeman's hand. His fingers opened wide and Remo pressed the stick against the base of the thumb, and the cop screeched with pain.

"Enough, enough," he yelled.

Remo kept pressing. "You a believer now?"

"Yes. I'm a believer."

"Oh no, not just a believer. Are you a true believer?"

"I is the truest believer."

"All right," Remo said, releasing his hand after one final squeeze. "Now cut out the 'chickenshit bullshit' and try to learn something."

So it went for the better part of the day, Remo — now McGurk's training officer — teaching the four policemen to defend themselves, to use force, to learn how to use that force to get information. He had been instructed by McGurk not to get into killing; these men were going to be investigators for the Men of the Shield when it "went public." They just had to be toughened.

It was boring work, lessons that Remo had mastered years ago in those first sessions with Chiun at Folcroft. Remo wondered why police departments spent all those federal funds buying tanks and foam sprayers and water cannons, none of which they ever used, instead of hiring somebody to teach their policemen to be effective. Maybe he and Chiun could incorporate. Go to work for the general public. Assassins Inc. Put an ad in the *Village Voice*. Defend yourself. Hassle a pig. They'd be rich. Chiun would be ecstatic. Think of all the money he could send back to Sinanju.

No, on the other hand, there was probably some reason why he couldn't do it. Some five-hundred-year-old proverb would make it impossible for Chiun to advertise in the *Voice* or to work for anyone except a government. Official assassins cannot work unofficially. That's that.

Another good idea shot to hell.

The training session lasted from 9:00 a.m. until noon. Occasionally, Remo saw McGurk stick his head out of the office in the rear of the big gym and watch Remo perform on the stage that had been erected in front of the firing dummy. McGurk would just watch, saying nothing, occasionally nodding in satisfaction, before pulling his head back inside.

It was close to lunchtime when Janet stuck her head out of the office. She moved into the doorway, wild and ripe in a short leather skirt and tight white sweater, and she crooked an imperious finger at Remo, directing him to her and Remo said, "Okay, men, that's enough for now. A long lunch and be back at two o'clock."

"Right. Okay. See you." They mumbled agreement and Remo hopped down off the stage and walked to the back where Janet O'Toole waited in the doorway.

"You called, madam?" he said.

"I called. And when I call, you come."

Remo looked down. "Many are called but not all come."

"That's because they haven't met *me*. Bill wants to talk to you," she said. "And when he's done, I think you and I ought to talk."

"Is the closet ready?"

Remo smiled at her, trying not to show his pleasure too openly. He had really brought the girl on. A week ago she was an emotional basket case. Now she was a tart. Was that plus one or minus one? Maybe it's what the political scientists called zero gain.

"What are you smiling about?" she demanded.

"You wouldn't understand."

"Try me," she said, and her tone was not inviting; it was cold and imperative.

"After I see McGurk," Remo said and walked past her, through her office, into McGurk's office in back. He was on the telephone and he motioned to Remo to shut the door and raised a finger to his mouth, cautioning Remo to be quiet.

Remo closed the door and stood inside, listening.

"No, sir," McGurk said.

"No," he said a moment later. "I've looked very carefully into the killing of Big Pearl. I can't find a thing that would support Congressman Duffy's killer cop theory."

And then, "No, sir, I wish I could. I'd like a crack at those bastards myself, but they just don't exist.

"Yessir, I'll keep looking. If there is such a thing, I'll find it. Yessir. After all, Duffy was my friend too.

"Bye."

He hung up the phone and smiled at Remo. "The Attorney General," he said. "Wondering if I've been able to find out anything about some kind of super-secret police killer organization. But of course I can't. There ain't any such animal."

"Naturally."

"Naturally."

McGurk smiled. "How's it going?"

"Great," Remo said. "As thrilling as watching ice melt. When's payday?"

"Tomorrow," McGurk said. "You'll get paid in full. Tomorrow."

He stood up behind his desk, after glancing at his watch. "Lunchtime," he said. "Join me?"

"No thanks," Remo said.

"Dieting?"

"Fasting."

"Keep your strength up. You'll need it," McGurk said.

Remo walked out with him and stood alongside as McGurk stopped at Janet's desk.

"Are you going to lunch or should I bring something back?" he asked.

She glanced at Remo, realized he was staying and asked McGurk to bring her back an egg salad sandwich and a chocolate milk shake.

The door had barely closed behind McGurk when Janet was on her feet, moving to the door and locking it.

She turned on Remo, her eyes glistening.

"I motioned to you this morning," she said.

"Yes?"

"And you ignored me. Why?"

"I didn't know you were calling. I thought you were just waving hello," Remo said.

"You're not supposed to think," she said. "You're supposed to be there when I call. Maybe some of those other women expect you to think, but I don't."

"I'm sorry," he said.

"You'll be sorrier," she said. "Take off your clothes."

Remo acted flustered. "Here? Now?"

"Here and now. Now! Hurry."

Remo obeyed, averting his eyes. All right, so he felt sorry for her but enough was about enough. Mental health wasn't really worth it. Just this one last time and then no more games.

Remo removed his slacks and shirt.

"I said all your clothes," she commanded.

He obeyed, Janet watching him, still standing with her back to the door.

When he was naked, standing amid his pile of clothing in the middle of the floor, she walked forward to him. She put her hands on his hips and looked into his eyes. He turned his face away.

"Now, take off my clothes," she said.

Remo reached behind her to begin pulling her sweater up over her head.

"Gently," she cautioned him. "Gently. If you know what's good for you."

———

Remo was not at home when the special telephone rang in the Folcroft office of Dr. Harold W. Smith.

With a sigh, Smith picked up the receiver.

"Yessir," he said.

"Has that person accomplished anything yet?" the familiar voice asked.

"He is occupied with it, sir."

"He has been occupied with it for one week," the voice said. "How long will this take?"

"It is difficult," Smith said.

"The Attorney General advises me that his efforts to find out anything about these assassination teams have been unsuccessful."

"As well they might be, sir," Smith said. "I would urge you to leave it to us."

"I am trying to do just that. But you realize, of course, that it is only a matter of time before the regular agencies of government become involved. And when they do, I will not be able simply to withdraw them. That could result in your organization being compromised."

"That is a risk we live with, sir."

"Please try to expedite things."

"Yessir."

And Remo was still not at home later that night when Smith called for the second time. He spoke instead to Chiun, probing, trying to find out if Remo might be dragging his feet on this assignment, still reluctant to go after policemen.

But Chiun was, as always, unfathomable on the telephone, answering only "yes" or "no" and finally, in exasperation, Smith said:

"Please give our friend a message."

"Yes," Chiun said.

"Tell him America is worth a life."

"Yes," Chiun said and hung up. He knew that years before, Conn MacCleary, the man who had recruited Remo, had told Remo that before asking Remo to kill him to preserve CURE's security.

Foolish white men. *Nothing* was worth a life.

There was only the purity of the art. All else was temporal and would too pass away. How foolish to worry about it.

And when Remo finally returned home, hours later, Chiun had decided not to tell him Smith had called.

CHAPTER EIGHTEEN

"TONIGHT'S THE NIGHT, REMO," McGurk said.

Remo lounged in the chair across from McGurk's desk.

"Tonight's what night?"

"The night we start making this a crime-free country." McGurk began to peel the paper from a small filter-tipped cigar. "When we start putting the policeman back on top where he belongs."

In the outer office, a mimeograph machine kerchugged as Janet O'Toole ran off press releases. Remo tested his ability to hear the cigar cellophane crinkle despite the overwhelming racket of the mimeography. He looked away so his ears would not be aided by his eyes watching the cellophane.

"Tonight, our forty-man core group is going to meet here at eight o'clock. I'll introduce you as our new training director. That'll only take a few minutes, and then we have a news conference slated for 9:30. All the press will be there, and we'll announce the formation of the Men of the Shield."

"You're not going to introduce *me* to the press?" Remo said.

He heard McGurk begin to roll the cellophane between his fingers, turning it into a hard little tube. "No," he said, "that's about all we don't need. No. Your involvement's going to be our own secret."

"Good, that's the way I like it," Remo said. He slid his chair back slightly, ready to stand.

"There's just one thing," McGurk said.

Remo sighed. "All my life, there's been just one thing."

"Yeah. Mine too. This one thing is important." McGurk stood and walked to the door. He opened it, assured himself that Janet was still working at the mimeograph machine, her ears outgunned by the noise. He closed the door tightly and returned to sit on the edge of the desk near Remo's feet.

"It's O'Toole," he said.

"What's with him?" Remo asked.

"He's ready to blow the whistle."

"Him? What the hell can he blow the whistle about?"

"I guess it's time to level with you, Remo," McGurk said. "This whole thing...the special teams...the Men of the Shield...the whole thing, it was all O'Toole's idea. "

"O'Toole? That psalm-singing liberal twit?"

"None other," McGurk said. "And now, like liberals always do, he's getting cold feet. He's told me if I don't cancel tonight, he'll expose the whole thing himself."

Remo nodded. That explained a lot of things, such as why McGurk, even though still a policeman, seemed to have all the time he needed to work on the Men of the Shield.

But O'Toole? Remo shook his head. "He'll never blow the whistle," he said.

"Why not?"

"Because it requires him to do something. Liberals are no good at that. They're good at talking, zero at doing."

"You're probably right, but we can't afford to take the chance. So..."

"So?"

"So you've got your first job."

"Quite a job," Remo said.

"Nothing you can't handle."

"When and where?"

McGurk went back behind his desk. He picked up the tube of cigar cellophane and began to fold it neatly into quarters.

"O'Toole's a creature of habit. Tonight, he always eats dinner at his home with Janet. Get him there. Dinner time. I've got the key to the place for you."

"And what about the girl?"

"I'll keep her here working late. She won't be around to bother you."

Remo thought a minute. "Okay," he said. "One last thing."

"Yeah?"

Remo rubbed his fingers together. "Cash."

"What's your going rate for this kind of a job?"

"For a police commissioner? Fifty big ones."

"You got it."

"In advance," Remo said.

"You got that too."

McGurk opened the safe on the other side of the room and took out a metal strongbox of money. He counted out fifty thousand and gave it to Remo who slid it inside his jacket pocket. "Another thing, McGurk. Why me? Why not one of your teams?"

"I want it done by one man. No teams. No involvements. And besides, it's a tough assignment to give a police team…to get another cop."

Remo nodded. He knew the feeling. It *was* hard to kill another cop. He stood up to leave. "Anything else?" he asked.

McGurk shook his head. He gave Remo a key and O'Toole's address. "Good luck," he offered.

"Luck has nothing to do with it."

McGurk watched him leave, then struck a match and lit his small cigar. He touched the match to the folded cellophane on the desk and watched it brown, bubble, and then burst into flame.

Outside, Remo realized that McGurk had not told him what he should do after the O'Toole hit. Well, no matter. He'd be back here for the eight o'clock meeting. It wouldn't do for the new training director not to show. He smiled appreciatively at Janet's mini-clad behind as he walked through the office, but she did not see or hear him leave.

There were three hours left before Remo had to go to O'Toole's house and he drove slowly back to his own home in the beige Fleetwood, thinking.

All along, through this case, he had been reluctant to go up against cops. But yet, when McGurk had told him to hit O'Toole, Remo had not even hesitated. But why? O'Toole was a cop too.

C'mon, Remo, is it because he's a liberal, and you like your cops to be straight, hard-line lapel-pinners?

No, it's not. I'm doing my job. O'Toole's the man behind this, and my job is to eliminate.

You don't really believe that, Remo. Stop trying to snow yourself. You don't even know for sure that O'Toole has anything to do with it. All you've got is McGurk's word, and that and twenty cents'll buy you a beer.

Remo argued with himself all the way to his home. He continued the argument while lying on the couch and Chiun watched him cautiously from the kitchen doorway.

It was moving on into late afternoon when Remo decided. He would go on the O'Toole job. But before he did anything, he would make sure for himself whether or not O'Toole was really the brains behind the Men of the Shield. If he wasn't, he lived. If he was, he died. That was the way it would be.

When Remo got up to leave, he was surprised to see that Chiun had changed from his white robe into a green garment of heavy brocade.

"Going somewhere?"

"Yes," Chiun said. "With you."

"There's no need for that," Remo said.

"All day long," Chiun said, "I stay in this house, cooking, cleaning, with no enjoyment, with no variety, while you are out having fun, teaching fools to be wonderful." His tone was petulant and whining.

"What's the matter with you, Chiun?"

"There is nothing the matter with the Master that will not be cured by getting out into the fresh air. Oh, to see the sky again, to feel the grass under my feet."

"There isn't any grass in this city. And no one's seen the sky for seven years."

"Enough of this bickering. I am going."

"All right, all right. But you stay in the car," Remo warned.

"Shall I bring a rope so you can tie me to the steering wheel?"

"No nonsense. You stay in the car."

And stay in the car Chiun did as Remo let himself into O'Toole's modest brick house with the key McGurk had given him.

Remo sat in the living room and watched the darkness settle over

New York. Out there in the city were thousands of criminals, thousands who would hurt and rob and maim and kill. Thousands, of whom only a fraction were ever caught and punished by the law. What made it so wrong if the police helped the law along? It was only what Remo himself did. Did he have a special permit because he was sanctioned by a higher agency of government? Was it a question of rank having its privileges, killing being one of them?

He looked around the room, at the mantel crowded with trophies, under a wall papered with plaques, the remnants of O'Toole's lifetime in police work.

No, he told himself. Remo and O'Toole were different. When Remo was assigned a job, it was that — a job. Not a vendetta, not the start of an unbroken string of assaults and killings. Just a job. But with the Men of the Shield, one killing must lead to another, one simple step following another simple step. It started out killing criminals. It graduated to a congressman. And now Remo was here, assigned by one cop to kill another cop.

Once the killing started, where was it checked? Who was to decide? The man with the most guns? Must it someday come to every man for himself, to the building of arsenals and armies? And he realized something that seemed forever to escape the changers of society: when the law was overturned, the land would be ruled by power. The rich and the strong and the guileful would survive, and the ones who would suffer most would be the poor and the weak, the very ones who screamed most for the system to be overthrown.

But the system must be preserved. And if it was entrusted to Remo Williams to preserve it, well, that was the biz, sweetheart.

Darkness was spreading when Remo heard the front door open, and then the soft footsteps padding down the hallway rug, and O'Toole entered the living room.

Remo stood up and said, "Good evening, O'Toole. I've come to kill you."

O'Toole looked at him in mild surprise, finally placed his face, and said: "The Mafia?"

"No. McGurk."

"That's what I would have guessed," O'Toole said. "It was only a matter of time."

"Once the killing starts," Remo said.

"Who's to finish it?"

"I'm afraid I am," Remo said. "You know why, don't you?"

"I do," O'Toole said. "Do you?"

"I think so. Because you're dangerous. A few more like you and this country won't survive."

"That's the right reason," O'Toole said. "But it's not why you're here. You're here because McGurk sent you and McGurk sent you because I'm the only one that stands in the way of his drive to political power."

"Come on," Remo said. "Political power. What's his platform? Bullets, not bullshit?"

"When he makes the Men of the Shield a pack of nationwide vigilantes...when he has every cop in America signed up...every police buff, every nit-nat flag waver, every right-wing racist, when he's got them all under the banner of that clenched fist, then he's got political power."

"He'll never see that day," Remo said.

"Will you stop him?"

"I'll stop him."

His eyes were locked on O'Toole who still stood just inside the doorway, talking softly with Remo. The police commissioner nodded, then said, "One thing."

"Name it."

"Can you make it look like the mob did it? If anyone ever learns about killer cops, it could destroy law enforcement in this country."

"I'll try," Remo said.

"For some reason, I trust you," O'Toole said. Remo moved slightly, instinctively, as O'Toole's hand went to his jacket pocket. He raised his hand. "Just a paper," he said, pulling out an envelope. "It's all in there. I'd rather go out as a cop killed by the enemies of the law, but if you need it, use it. It's in my handwriting. There'll be no argument about its authenticity."

He walked to the bar and poured himself a drink. "It started so simply," he said, draining the glass of Scotch. "Just getting the men who got my daughter. It was so simple at the start."

"It always is," Remo said. "It always starts simple. All tragedies do."

And then, because there was nothing else to say, Remo killed

O'Toole in his living room, killed him gently and quickly, and carefully placed his body on the living room rug.

He sat back down in a chair and in the dying light opened the envelope O'Toole had given him. It was filled with ten sheets of paper, typed single-spaced, and it gave names and places and dates. It told how he and McGurk had planned the national assassination squads; how they had recruited men around the country from among their personal friends in police work; it told of Congressman Duffy's death; of McGurk's plan to form the Men of the Shield; of McGurk's growing political lust and how it finally became apparent to O'Toole that McGurk figured himself to be the man on the white horse that America traditionally looked for. And it told how O'Toole had tried to stop it but had lost control.

Each page was signed and the cover sheet was written by hand. As he read it, Remo realized why O'Toole had faced death so calmly. The note was a suicide note; he had planned to take his own life.

Remo read the note twice, feeling through the words O'Toole's anguish and pain. When he finished the second time, his eyes were wet.

O'Toole had lived like a shit, Remo thought. But he had died like a man. And that was more than most men got. It was something.

It was a better death than McGurk would have. In another forty-five minutes, McGurk would be meeting with his cadre of killer cops. Well, they would just have to stay out of it. Remo hoped they would.

CHAPTER NINETEEN

REMO MOVED QUICKLY. With luck, he could get to the gym on Twentieth Street before the meeting started. Finish McGurk. End the Men of the Shield before they ever had a chance to start.

His preoccupation overwhelmed his senses and then he realized he was not alone.

They had moved in behind Remo as he left O'Toole's house and one called: "Bednick." Remo turned. There were three of them. Obviously policemen in plain clothes. They wore their occupation like banners.

He was in trouble. He knew they would not have moved in behind him unless they had people cutting off his exit at the gate. He glanced over his shoulder. There were three more. Each carried a weapon, professionally, held back close to the hip. Six cops sent to kill him. He had been played for a sucker by McGurk, and had fallen into the trap.

"Bednick?" one of the men near the house said again.

"Who wants to know?" Remo said. He moved closer to the house, hoping to draw the three men behind him up closer, close enough to work by hand.

"We want to know," the cop said. "The Men of the Shield."

"Sorry, pal, I gave at the office," Remo said.

He took another step forward and heard the shuffling behind him as the line moved up closer to him.

"McGurk said you had to die."

"McGurk. You know he's using you?"

The cop laughed.

"And we're wasting you," he said. Then he was pulling back the hammer on his pistol. He raised his hand to eye level, drew dead aim on Remo, and then he was falling to the ground, as out of the night, with a chilling shriek, came Chiun, dropping down onto the men from above. He landed among the three men and Remo took advantage of the moment of shock to move backwards into the bodies of the three behind him. He worked left and right, and behind him he could hear the terrible sound of Chiun's blows, like whip cracks, and he knew he could save none of those men. But there was one still alive near Remo. He gasped as Remo leaned on his throat. His gun had fallen from his hand and lay out of reach.

"Quick," Remo said. "Were you supposed to report back to McGurk?"

"Yeah."

"To tell him you got me?"

"Yeah."

"How?"

"Phone him at his office. Let the phone ring two times and then hang up."

"Thanks, pal," Remo said. "You won't believe it but together, you and me, we're going to save the police profession in this country."

"You're right, Bednick, I *don't* believe it."

"That's the biz, sweetheart," Remo said, and then put him to sleep forever.

He stood up and looked at Chiun who stood silently, porcelain delicate, among the bodies strewn around the walkway.

"Taking inventory?" Remo asked.

"Yes. Eight idiots gone. Remaining: the Master of Sinanju and one more idiot. You."

"No more, Chiun. Come on, we've got an appointment."

As they walked down the drive, Remo asked, "You saw them coming and you climbed the roof, right?"

Chiun snarled at him. "Do you think the Master of Sinanju climbs roofs like a chimney sweep? I sensed their presence. And I entered among them and I swooped to the right and I swooped to the left; like the wind on fire I moved among them, and when the Master was done, he was alone with death. He had brought death out of the night sky onto the evil men."

"In other words, you jumped on them from the roof."

"From the roof," Chiun agreed.

Later, in the car, Remo told Chiun that he had been right. "But I'm over it now. No more good guy, bad guy for me."

"I am happy that you have found the remnants of your reason. Doctor Smith sent a message to you."

"Oh?"

"Yes. He said America is worth a life."

"When'd he call?"

"I don't remember," Chiun said. "I am not your Kelly girl."

Remo chuckled. "Thanks for not telling me until I was ready."

"Nonsense," Chiun said. "I merely forgot."

CHAPTER TWENTY

THE TELEPHONE RANG ONCE ON the desk of Inspector William McGurk. Instinctively, his hand reached for it, but he checked himself and waited. The phone rang again. He waited. The phone rang no more.

McGurk smiled. All the loose ends were coming into place. No more O'Toole to worry about. No more Remo Bednick to stand between him and Janet. He was glad he had gotten rid of the girl. She was on a plane now to Miami, supposedly at her father's request. It would be better for her to be spared some of the close-up tragedy.

Outside his office, McGurk could hear the policemen milling around and he glanced at his watch. Eight p.m. Almost time to begin. His meeting would have to be over in time for the 9:30 press conference. But that meeting was for the press and the public. This one was private. For the police who made up McGurk's army.

McGurk picked up the sheets of paper on his desk. Carefully typed sheets. The speech he had been working on for so long. But he would not deliver it tonight. He had important news that took precedence over any formal speech. Well, he'd get some of it in anyway.

The thing was foolproof. He would explain to the men the terrible tragedy that had befallen the cause of law enforcement; he would let them know that they were the elite shock troops of thousands who would come after; he would announce his plans for a private investigation force against crime; he would let them know, without ever saying it, that they were entering a period when the assassination teams would lie quiet for a while. And without their ever realizing it, he would tie them to him politically, as the first step in his plan to gain political power.

McGurk stood up and looked out into the big gym room. Christ, policemen were noisy. There was a crowd around the table with the liquor; the table with the sandwiches was deserted. The forty men in the room sounded like four hundred.

He stepped through Janet's empty office and paused in the doorway to the gym. He caught the eyes of two men who stood at the large steel doors leading to the hallway and nodded. They were his sergeants-at-arms. The thought made him chuckle. One was a deputy police chief from Chicago, the other an inspector from Los Angeles. Sergeants-at-arms. They had made sure that no one but Men of the Shield entered the room. Now they would turn away company until the meeting was over.

The heavy doors swung shut behind the men who took up their positions in the outside hallway, and McGurk moved out to start greeting the policemen.

Remo had hung up the telephone after two rings, jumped back in the car and began the maddening drive crosstown to McGurk's headquarters.

"Drive right," Chiun said.

"I *am* driving right. If you don't drive like a kamikaze pilot, they know you're from out of town and they terrorize you." Remo swerved between two cars, giving one driver an attack of nerves, and clearing the other's sinuses.

"It is not necessary for them to terrorize me," Chiun said. "You are perfectly equipped for the task. "

"Dammit, Chiun, do you want to drive?"

"No, but if I did want to drive, I would do it with a sense of responsibility to the men of Detroit who have managed to build this vehicle so well it has not yet fallen apart."

"Next time, walk. Who invited you anyway?"

"I need no invitation. But are you not glad that the Master was there when you needed him?"

"Right on, Chiun, yeah, yeah, yeah."

"Insolent."

It seemed like forever, but actually it was only minutes later when they pulled into a parking spot at a fire hydrant near the building on Twentieth Street.

They were met at the top of the stairs by McGurk's two doormen.

"Sorry, men," the taller one said. "Private meeting now. No one allowed without authorization."

"That's ridiculous," Remo said. "We were invited here by McGurk."

"Yeah?" the police officer said suspiciously. His hand went to an inside pocket and took out a list of names.

"What are your names?" he asked.

"I'm S. Holmes. This is C. Chan."

The officer scanned the list quickly. "Where are you from?"

"We're with Hawaii Five-Oh."

"Oh."

"No. Five-Oh," Remo corrected.

"Let me see." The policeman looked down again at the sheet. His partner looked with him.

Remo raised his hands and brought them down fingers first into their collarbones. The two men dropped.

"Adequate," Chiun said.

"Thank you. I didn't want you to go killing them," Remo said. "For at least a week after you have duck, you're uncontrollable."

He opened the door and dragged the two unconscious men inside, into the small foyer. He checked to make sure they would be out for at least an hour, then propped them in a sitting position against the wall.

He snapped the lock behind him and Chiun, sealing anyone else outside.

He and Chiun paused at the glass, looking inside the room. Remo spotted McGurk immediately, moving through the small clusters of policemen, shaking a hand here, patting a shoulder there, but moving steadily toward the small stage at the front of the hall.

"That's him," Remo said pointing. "McGurk."

Chiun sipped in his breath. "He is an evil man."

"Now, how the hell can you say that? You don't even know him."

"One can tell by the face. Man is a peaceable creature. He must be taught to kill. He must be given a reason. But this one? Look at his eyes. He likes to kill. I have seen eyes like those before."

The crowd was now drifting toward the folding wooden chairs that had been set up. Remo said, "Chiun, you're a sweet guy and all but you just don't look like a detective sergeant from Hoboken. You'd better stay out here while I go inside."

"Whistle if you need me."

"Right."

"You know how to whistle? Just put your lips together and blow."

"You've been watching *The Late Show* again."

"Go earn your keep," Chiun commanded.

Remo slipped inside the heavy door and moved easily into the flow of the crowd, drifting into a group of men headed for seats in the back. He kept his chin burrowed down into his chest and changed his gait to make identification more difficult, in case McGurk should be looking his way. Most of the men in the room were still wearing their hats. He picked one up from a folding chair and planted it on his head, pulling it down to shield his eyes, lest McGurk spot them.

McGurk was now at the base of the stairs leading to the stage. He took the steps in a bound and then stood, without a microphone, in front of the men, signaling them by his silence that it was time to sit down and listen.

Slowly, the forty men settled into the seventy-five chairs. Assassins from all over the country, Remo thought, and then changed his mind. No. Not assassins. Just men who were fed up with the obstacles society threw in their way when they were trying to do a job. Just men who believed in law and order so much that, foolishly, they would go outside the law to secure it. McGurk's dupes.

McGurk raised his hands for silence. The babbling drifted off into a stillness that hung over the room.

"Men of the Shield," McGurk said deeply, "welcome to New York."

He looked slowly around the room.

"This is a proud moment for me, but a deeply sorrowful one too. I'm proud because I am meeting with you men, the finest policemen — no, let me say cops because the word doesn't embarrass me — the finest cops in our nation...men who have put their lives on the line many times in the never-ending struggle for law and order in our land. And men...I don't have to remind you...who have made that extra special commitment that few others have the courage to make.

"In a little more than an hour, the press is going to be in here and I'm going to tell the nation about the formation of the Men of the Shield. I'm going to tell them how we will become a national clearinghouse to solve the crimes that plague our cities and make our streets unsafe. Already I have information" — he paused and chuckled slightly — "on several of the more dastardly crimes that have been committed in the current wave of violence that has hit the country."

He chuckled again and this time several policemen joined in.

"And let me tell you this," McGurk said. "The criminals responsible for those crimes will be punished. And that will show that the Men of the Shield mean business. And from that moment on, our goal will be to bring every policeman and every law enforcement officer in the country under our banner; so that together we can get on with the job of stamping out crime. When the politicians won't act, when the prosecutors turn their heads, when the bleeding hearts try to stop the law, the Men of the Shield will be there, investigating, finding the truth and forcing society to bring to bear its full weight against the evil-doers in our land."

Remo smiled to himself. So that's what it was all about. Planting clues at the scene of a crime, then planting the evidence on someone they wanted to hang. A quick, easy way to get a national reputation and, in the process, get rid of a couple of baddies. Well planned, McGurk.

"The first phase of our work is, I believe, now behind us." McGurk paused and cleared his throat significantly. "Let's call it our planning and preparation phase." He grinned, showing long yellow teeth. Remo saw the policemen in the room grin and turn toward each other. There was a hum of words, and McGurk spoke over them.

"So it is with pride that I meet with you tonight, as we embark on this long journey forward into a day when our nation will be free again from the chains of crime, when our wives and children will be safe in their beds, when every street in every city in every corner of our country will be safe to walk at any hour of the day or night. And if, to accomplish that takes more than police investigation, if it takes political power, then I say the Men of the Shield will pursue that political power and we will use it with all our united strength."

"Right on."

"You said it."

There were scattered shouts of approval around the room.

McGurk let the noise continue for a moment, then began to speak softly.

"That is why I stand here with pride. But as I said, I come in sadness too. I have been delivered a blow of such sadness that I honestly thought of canceling this meeting.

"I have just been informed that the police commissioner of this city, Commissioner O'Toole...the man, more than any other who was responsible for the formation of the Men of the Shield...the man who has been at my side during these long hours...I have just learned that Commissioner O'Toole has been murdered in his home."

He paused to let his words sink in. There was a quick-lived buzz of words, and then all heads turned toward McGurk for more information.

"But I decided to go on with the meeting anyway because I think the tragic death of the commissioner underscores the need for our organization."

"How'd he get it?" one man shouted.

"He was killed in his home," McGurk said, "by an infamous Mafia thug in this city...a paid killer for organized crime...a man who even tried to infiltrate our own police department...a sewer of evil named Remo Bednick. But fortunately, Bednick is dead from the bullets of our city's finest.

"As I said, I thought of shutting down this meeting because of this terrible tragedy, but then I realized that Commissioner O'Toole would have wanted it to be held, to show to you men the terrible risks we must take as an organization if you men are brave enough to accept the challenge of standing up to the forces of organized crime."

McGurk pulled his wallet from his pocket, and opened it, showing the badge Remo had first seen in Captain Milken's wallet.

"This is the badge of the Men of the Shield," McGurk said. "It was designed personally by Commissioner O'Toole. I hope and pray that each of us will carry it with honor and pride as we set off now on our long crusade to insure that never again will a policeman die from a gangster's gun."

He stood there, holding the badge up over his head. The gold glinted almost dark brown in the overhead fluorescent lights, and McGurk rotated the badge slowly, letting it flash, milking the drama of the moment, as the policemen watched him silently, and finally Remo stood up in the last row quietly, his hat still pulled down over his eyes, and he called out briskly into the silence:

"McGurk. You're a yellow-bellied lying bastard."

CHAPTER TWENTY-ONE

THERE WAS A STARTLED RUMBLE in the room as Remo moved down the aisle toward McGurk.

He still wore the hat and he walked heavily on his feet so McGurk would not recognize the smooth glide with which Remo usually moved.

Remo stood at the bottom of the small stage, looking down, and then he raised his head slowly and met McGurk's eyes. McGurk's expression had been one of mystified interest, but now it turned to shock when he saw and recognized the man he knew as Remo Bednick.

Remo stared at him coldly, then turned and faced the crowd of police officers who were still buzzing, watching the strange confrontation.

Remo silenced them by raising a hand.

"I want to read you something Commissioner O'Toole wrote," he said.

He pulled the papers from his pocket and shuffled through them, finally pulling out the sheet that O'Toole had written.

"O'Toole was a sick man," Remo said. "He had started something and then seen it get away from him. He had seen it turned into something designed to promote the interests, not of law and order, but of one man, and one man only.

"He planned suicide, and this note was to be his last will and

127

testament. He told everything in it. How he had started the Men of the Shield to fight crime, and how he had tried to stop it from being turned into a political organization. And then he failed. And so he wrote: 'And so I am putting down these notes so that the authorities, properly alerted, can take the steps that will guarantee that our nation will continue as a nation of law, working as free men, together, under the Constitution.

"'And even more, I am addressing these words to the policemen of this country, that thin blue line that represents all that stands between us and the jungle. I do this secure in the knowledge that when the facts are presented to them, they will do as policemen have done since time immemorial — they will face and meet their responsibilities; they will act as free men and not as political pawns in a huckster's evil shell game; they will stand tall as Americans.

"'To achieve that end, my death may give to me a worth that the last acts of my life have denied me.'"

Remo stopped and looked into the stillness around the room, meeting the eyes of the policemen sitting there. Behind him, on the stage, McGurk began to shout: "Liar! Liar! Forgery! Don't believe him, men."

Remo turned and leaped up onto the stage, tossing his hat onto the small table behind McGurk.

He turned again toward the crowd. "No, it's true," he shouted, "and I'll tell you how I know. I know because I killed O'Toole. I killed him because I was sent to kill him. And who sent me? Why, that noble friend of policemen everywhere. Inspector William McGurk. Because O'Toole wouldn't let him use you men to become a political power."

"You're a liar," McGurk roared.

Remo turned toward him. McGurk reached in under his jacket and pulled out a revolver.

Remo looked at him and smiled. "Is there anything worse than a cop-killer?" he shouted. "Yes," he answered himself. "A *cop* who's a cop-killer, and that's what McGurk is."

He turned toward McGurk. The revolver was leveled now at Remo's chest. McGurk's eyes were as cold as jagged glass.

"Remember those men on my front porch, McGurk?" Remo asked. "If you want to try pulling that trigger, go ahead."

"Tell them the truth, Bednick," McGurk said. "Tell them that you're a Mafia button man who was assigned to kill our commissioner."

"I would," Remo said, "but you and I know that it's not true. I worked for you. And I killed Commissioner O'Toole for you. Come on, McGurk. You've made a reputation by how tough and hard you are. That's all these men have heard about for years. Show them now. Pull that trigger."

He was three feet from McGurk and his eyes burned into McGurk's with the kind of heat that could melt glass. McGurk saw in his mind the ambush he had set for Remo and the dead men in the yard; he thought now of the six dead men who must be lying in O'Toole's yard; he thought of the smell of death that Remo seemed to carry with him.

"Pull that trigger, McGurk," Remo said. "And when you're dying, very slowly, these men are going to take the badges of the Men of the Shield and drop them on your body. You made a real mistake, McGurk. You took them for fools, because they were cops. But they're smarter than you are. Sure, one of every two slobs they catch gets off. But you've been selling them short. They know the rules are tough because they have to be. If the rules weren't tough, McGurk, a slob like you might be running this country — a cop-killing slob who isn't worth an honest cop's spit. Go ahead, McGurk. Try to pull that trigger."

Through it all, Remo smiled at McGurk and McGurk finally recognized where he had seen that hard smile before, a smile that looked like a rip in a piece of silk. It had been on Remo's face when he killed that last cop in his front yard, a cruel painful smile that spoke volumes about pain and torture.

The gun barrel wavered momentarily, and then in a flash McGurk raised the revolver to his temple and squeezed. The report was muffled by flesh and bone and McGurk's scream. He dropped heavily to the stage. The gun clattered loose from his fingertips as they opened. It bounced once and came to a rest a few feet from his body. As he fell, the pages of his speech slipped from his jacket pocket and slowly fluttered down onto his body.

Remo picked up the gun, looked at it, then tossed it on the table. He turned again to the policemen who sat in their seats as if cemented there, trying to absorb the incredible events of the last few minutes.

"Men," Remo said, "go home. Forget McGurk and forget me and

forget the Men of the Shield. Just remember, when you get to thinking that your job is tough, that, of course, it is. That's why America picked its best men to be cops. That's why so many people are proud of you. Go home."

He started to speak again, but Chiun had stepped quietly inside the door and now raised an index finger to his mouth, as if to shush Remo.

Softly, Remo said again, his voice slowly trailing off, "Go home."

And then he jumped from the stage and strode purposefully up the aisle, past the rows of men on each side. He paused with Chiun at the door and looked back.

From the audience, men were tossing badges toward the stage, where they hit, or bounced near, McGurk's body.

Remo turned and walked through the doors.

"You did well, my son," Chiun said.

"Yeah. And I make me sick."

CHAPTER TWENTY-TWO

WHEN REMO TELEPHONED IN, he gave Smith the full report. O'Toole's death. The cops who had been sent to ambush Remo and had died. McGurk's suicide.

"How the hell are we going to explain all that?" Smith asked.

"Look," Remo said angrily. "You wanted this thing broken up. It's broken up. How you pick up the loose ends is your business. Send a special team from the Attorney General's office to investigate and later bring in a whitewash of the whole thing."

"And what about the members of the Men of the Shield? The assassination teams?"

"Forget them," Remo said. "They're just cops who made a mistake."

"I want their names," Smith said. "They're killers."

"So am I. You can have them the day after you come for me."

"That day may come," Smith said.

"Que sera, sera," Remo said and hung up.

End of report.

But he still had not told Smith everything, and an hour later he was on a plane to Miami, to see if there was one last loose end he had personally failed to tie up.

Smith had triggered it when he had talked about the computer efficiency of a nationwide killing operation manned by only forty people. O'Toole had mentioned it when he talked of his reasons for launching the Men of the Shield. McGurk had lent weight to it once when he described Janet O'Toole as "the brains of the operation."

Remo had to find out if it was true. Had Janet O'Toole, the computer expert, been part and parcel of the plan to kill, because of her insane hatred of all men? He had to find out because if she was, neatness demanded that she be taken care of.

He found her at the Inca Motel, a dismaying straggle of buildings and pools with varying pollution counts. She was sipping a tall drink at midnight near an outside pool when Remo arrived.

He stood outside the glare of the ring of lights and watched her, sprawled languorously in a beach chair.

The busboy brought a drink up to her and while he stood there with it in his hand, she stretched like a cat, arching her back, thrusting her breasts upward toward the boy.

Finally, she took the drink, but as the boy was walking away, she froze him in mid-stride by calling imperiously:

"Boy!"

"Yes, ma'am?"

"Come here," she said. The boy was in his early twenties, blond and tan and good-looking. He stopped at her feet looking down at her, and she pulled up her knees, spreading her legs slightly, and asked him softly, "Why have you been staring at me?"

She wore a tiny two-piece bikini and the youth stammered and said, "Well...I...I didn't...I..."

"Don't lie," she said. "You did. Is there something I have that other women don't have?" Before he could answer, she said, "I'm tired of your insolence. I'm going to my room. I want you there in five minutes and you'd better be prepared to explain your behavior."

She set her glass on the pool deck, stood up and walked away gracefully on high spiked heels.

Remo waved the boy to him.

"What's with her?" he asked.

The youth grinned. "She's a sex fiend, Mister. It's how she gets her kicks. She's been here only a couple of hours and she's balled half the staff. First she chews them out, and then drags us to the room and... well, you know."

"Yeah, I know," Remo said, then leaned forward and gave the youth a hundred-dollar bill.

Janet O'Toole was naked when the knock on the door came a few minutes later. She turned off her light and pulled the door open slightly.

A male figure stood there. He said softly, "I've come to apologize."

"Come in, you evil-minded child, you. I'm going to have to punish you, you know."

She took the man's hand and pulled him into the room. A moment later, their bodies were locked together.

But in her brief career as courtesan, it had never been like this. The man brought her to heights, higher and higher, until she felt like skin-covered jelly.

She reached a peak and the voice whispered in her ear, "Your father's dead."

"Who cares? Don't stop."

"So's McGurk."

"Keep going. The hell with McGurk."

"The Men of the Shield are disbanded."

"So what? Just another bullshit organization anyway. Keep it coming."

He did.

When Remo got up later, she was sleeping, her mouth opened slightly, her breath still coming fast and shallow.

He flipped on the dresser light and looked at her. No, he decided, she wasn't a killer, just a computer operator. The only way she'd ever try to kill a man was in bed, in a fashion allowed by law.

Remo stood at the small dresser, took paper and pen from the center drawer, and wrote a quick note.

Dear Janet:

Sorry, but you're too much woman for me.

- *Remo.*

He left the note on her bare breasts, and went out into the Miami heat.

THE END

EXCERPT

If you enjoyed *Murder's Shield*, maybe you'll like *Terror Squad*, too. It's the tenth Destroyer novel, now available in paperback and as an ebook.

Terror Squad

HIS NAME WAS REMO, and he did not feel very special.

He felt incredibly ordinary that bright California morning, standing beside his sky-blue pool, just like any other pool, near any other luxury villa in this luxury community in a luxury county where everyone talked about his stock investments, or the movie he was making, or the bitch of an income tax.

Did Remo find the new tax bill threatening? He was asked this often at the ordinary cocktail parties made ordinary by their repetition and the dull ordinariness of the people attending them who invariably felt, for some strange reason, that they were extraordinary.

No, Remo did not find the new tax bill threatening.

Would Remo care for a cocktail? A joint? A pill?

No, Remo did not indulge.

An hors d'oeuvre?

No, it might have monosodium glutamate and Remo ate only once a day anyhow.

Was Remo a health food addict?

No, his body was.

The face was familiar. Did Remo make a flick in Paris?

No. Perhaps they just used the same plastic surgeon.

Just what did Remo do for a living?

Suffered fools gladly.

Would Remo care to repeat that statement out on the terrace?

Not really.

Did Remo know he was speaking to the former amateur light heavyweight champion of California and a black belt holder, not to mention the heavy mob connections anyone owning a studio would have?

Remo did not realize all that.

Would Remo care to repeat that statement about fools?

The fool had done it for him.

How would Remo like an hors d'oeuvre in his face?

That would be quite impossible because the silver hors d'oeuvre tray was going to be wrapped around the fool's head.

Remo remembered that last cocktail party he had attended in Beverly Hills, how two servants had to hammer and chisel the tray from the movie mogul's head, how the movie mogul complained directly to Washington, even used his influence to get government agencies to check out Remo's background. They found nothing, of course. Not even a Social Security number. Which was natural. Dead men have neither Social Security numbers nor fingerprints on file.

Remo stuck a toe into the too-blue water. Lukewarm. He glanced back at the house where the wide glass patio doors were open. He heard the morning soap operas grinding into their teary beginnings. Suddenly a voice cut through the television organ music.

"Are you ready? I'll be listening," came a squeaky, Oriental voice from inside the house.

"Not ready yet, Little Father," said Remo.

"You should always be ready."

"Yeah. Well, I'm not," yelled Remo.

"A wonderful answer. A full explanation. A rational cause."

"Well, I'm just not ready yet. That's all."

"…for a white man," came the squeaky Oriental voice.

"For a white man," hissed Remo testily under his breath.

He tried the water with the other foot. Still lukewarm.

There had been flack from headquarters over the hors d'oeuvre tray incident.

Was Remo aware of the incredible jeopardy he had placed the agency in by attracting attention?

Remo was aware.

Did Remo know the effect on the nation if the existence of the agency should become known?

Remo knew.

Did Remo know the expense and risk the agency had gone to in establishing him as a man without living identity?

If Dr. Harold W. Smith, head of CURE, was referring to framing a policeman named Remo Williams for murder, getting the policeman sentenced to the electric chair so that when the switch was pulled and the body pronounced dead the prints would be destroyed and the Social Security number removed, and the poor guy would no longer exist, if that's what Dr. Smith meant, yes, Remo remembered very well all the trouble CURE had gone to.

And all the trouble with the never-ending training that had turned him into something other than a normal human being, Remo remembered well.

He remembered a lot of things. Believing he was going to be executed and waking up in a hospital bed. Being told that the Constitution was in peril and a President had authorized an agency to have powers to fight crime beyond constitutional limits. A secret organization that would not exist. Only the President; Dr. Harold W. Smith, the head of the secret organization CURE; the recruiter; and Remo would ever know. And of course Remo was a dead man, having been executed the night before for murder.

Still, there had been a little problem when the recruiter got injured and lay drugged in a hospital bed, perhaps ready in his narcotic fog to talk about CURE. But that little matter was easily taken care of. Remo, the dead policeman, was ordered to kill him and then there were only three people who knew of CURE.

Why only one man for the enforcement arm of CURE? the ex-Remo Williams had asked.

Less chance of CURE becoming a threat to the government. Of course, the one man would get special training.

And he did — training from the Master of the House of Sinanju, training so extreme at times that even a real death seemed preferable.

Yes, Remo remembered all the trouble CURE had gone to for him, and if wrapping a tray around a fool's head endangered all that work, well, that was the business, sweetheart.

"Is that all you can say, Remo? That's the biz?" Dr. Smith had said in one of those rare face-to-face meetings.

"That's all I can say."

"Well, it's done," said the lemon-faced Dr. Smith. "Now to the business at hand. What do you know about terrorists?" Then followed an afternoon briefing on terrorists, a preamble to a mission.

Remo bent over and tinkled a hand in the pool like everyone else's pool in this luxury community.

"I do not hear a body move through the water," came the Oriental voice.

"I do not hear a body move through the water," Remo mimicked under his breath. He stood in boxer bathing trunks, an apparently normally built man in his early thirties with sharp features and deep dark eyes. Only his thick wrists would give any indication that this was more than an ordinary man, for the real deadliness was where it always is with man, in his mind.

"I do not hear a body move through the water," came the voice again.

Remo went into the pool. Not in a dive or a splashing jump, but instead, the way he had been taught, like the essence of gravity returning toward the center of the earth. Even a novice in the martial arts knew that collapsing was actually the fastest way of getting down. This was an extension of it. One moment, Remo was standing on the side of the pool, and the next, the lukewarm water surrounded him, above him, and around him, and his feet were on tile. To someone watching, it would appear as if the pool just sucked him in.

He waited, letting his eyes adjust to the stinging chlorinated water, letting his restricted use of oxygen adjust his body, letting the arms float while the mind concentrated the focus of the weight at his feet and legs to keep him steady underwater,

He was in a world of warm blue jade and he adjusted to become part of it, not fight it. When he had first learned moving through water, he had tried harder and harder, and succeeded less and less. The Master of Sinanju, Chiun, had said that when he stopped trying he would learn to move through water, and that it was Remo's arrogance that made him believe he could overpower it, instead of submitting to it.

"By submission, you conquer," Chiun had said, and then demonstrated.

The wisp of an aged Oriental had entered the water properly, leaving a trail of only three small bubbles following the descent of his body, as if a small rock had been placed gently, not dropped, into the water. Without seeming propulsion, the body suddenly was moving through the water much as Remo had seen a tiger shark do in a city aquarium back east. No flailing. No straining. Swish. Swish. Swish. And Chiun was at the other end of the pool and out of the water as though vacuumed out. It was the training of the House of Sinanju that made its masters appear not to push themselves but to be pulled.

Remo had tried. Failed. Tried again. Failed. Until one tired afternoon, following three failures in which he had moved no better than an ordinary swimmer, he felt the tuning of his body.

His body in conjunction with the water made the forward movement. It was too easy to believe. And then, trying it again, he found he could not do it again.

Chiun had leaned over the pool and taken Remo's hand. He pushed it against the water. Remo felt force. Then he pulled Remo's hand through the water. The hand moved swiftly, without effort. The water accepted the hand.

That was the key.

"Why didn't you show me this the first time?" Remo had asked.

"Because you did not know what you did not know. You had to begin at ignorance."

"Little Father," Remo had said, "you're as clear as scripture."

"But your testaments are not clear at all," Chiun had said. "And I am very clear. Unfortunately, a light to a blind man is always inadequate. You now know how to move through water."

And Chiun was right. Remo never failed again. Now, as he unweighted his feet, he understood the water, its very nature, and he too moved, not cutting through but blending the weight thrusts of his body with the mass of the water to pull himself forward. Swish. Swish. Swish. Up and out of the pool, then stroll back, leaving wet footprints on the yellow outdoor rag. It was not exercise, because exercise meant straining the body. This was practice.

Once more, down into the pool and off — swish, swish, swish. Then up and out and pad back to the beginning. On the third time, Remo glanced quickly back to the house. Competence had already brought him to the point of boredom. To hell with it. He slapped the water once at one end, dashed to the other and slapped it again.

"Perfect," came the Oriental voice. "Perfect. The first time you have achieved perfection. For a white man, that is."

It was only that evening when Chiun's television shows were over, and Remo continued to maintain a happy little secret smile, that Chiun looked quizzically at his pupil and said:

"That third moving through the water was false."

"What, Little Father?"

"False. You cheated."

"Would I do that?" asked Remo indignantly.

"Would the spring rice swallow the dew of the Yucca bird?"

"Would it? I don't know," Remo said. "I never heard of a Yucca bird."

"You know. You cheated. You are too happy for having paid the proper effort in this morning's training. But I say to you, whoever robs from his own efforts robs himself. And in our craft, the robber's price can well be death."

The telephone rang, interrupting the aged Oriental. Chiun, casting a baleful eye upon the ringing instrument, became quiet, as if unwilling to compete with a machine so insolent it would dare interrupt him. Remo picked up the receiver.

"This is Western Union," came the voice. "Your Aunt Alice is coming to visit you and wants you to prepare the guest room."

"Right," Remo said. "But what color guest room?"

"Just the guest room."

"Are you sure?"

"That's what it says, sir," said the Western Union operator, with the smug arrogance of one observing another's discomfort.

"Just guest room. Not blue guest room or red guest room?"

"Correct, sir. I will read…"

Remo hung up on the Western Union operator, waited the few moments necessary for a dial tone, then dialed again, an 800 area-code number that he was ordered to call because the telegram did not mention the guest room's color.

The phone barely rang once and was answered.

"Remo, we're in luck. We got them 2,000 feet over Utah. Remo, this is you, right?"

"Well, yes it is. It would help to have you verify before you start vomiting over an open line. What the hell is the matter with you, Smitty?" Remo was shocked. Smith's external composure was usually perfect, almost Korean.

"We got a whole crew of them over Utah. They want ransom money. Federal agencies are negotiating now. The money delivery will be at Los Angeles Airport. See an FBI field representative, Peterson. He's a black man. You will be the negotiator. Jump the line to the top. This is the first lead we've had. Repeat for verify."

"See Peterson at Los Angeles Airport. Board the plane and try to find out who the leaders are of this whole thing. I assume this is an airline hijacking," Remo said drily.

"Beautiful. Get going now. You may not have time to lose."

Remo hung up.

"What is the matter?" asked Chiun.

"Dr. Harold Smith, our employer, has taken a mental leap off a cliff. I don't know what's the matter," said Remo, his face twisted in concern.

"You'll be working tonight, then?" Chiun said.

"Ummmm," said Remo, signifying assent. "Gotta go now."

"Wait. I might go with you. It might be a nice evening."

"Barbra Streisand's on tonight, Chiun."

"This thing you do cannot be done tomorrow night?"

"No."

"Good luck. And remember when you are tempted to take risks, think of all the hours I have invested in you. Think of the nothing you were and the level to which I have raised you."

"I'm pretty good, huh, Little Father?" said Remo, regretting the comment as soon as he made it.

"For a white man," Chiun said happily.

"Your mother is a Wasoo," yelled Remo, dashing out the door. He was across the yard and into the garage before he realized the Master of Sinanju was not chasing him. He did not know what a Wasoo was, but Chiun had used the word once in a very rare moment of anger.

The Rolls Royce Silver Cloud was the car parked closest to the garage door. It didn't really matter which car Remo drove or even owned. He didn't own anything. He only used things. He didn't even own his face which, every so often, especially if anyone should accidentally get a photograph, was changed by plastic surgery. He owned nothing and had the use of practically anything he wanted. Like the Rolls Royce, he thought, backing up the Silver Cloud, its magnificently honed motor humming quietly, moving effortlessly, a paramount achievement in its field — like Remo, the Destroyer, a testimonial to manufacturing skills.

As usual, the airport traffic was insufferable, but that was America and there were some things even training couldn't overcome. Unless, of course, he wanted to run over car roofs to get to the airport. He watched the sun set bloody red through its filter of pollution and knew that somewhere above him an airplane was heading for Los Angeles Airport with terrified people on board, being held as hostages by the hijackers. To some people it was a moment of terror. To the professional, it was only a link in a chain, and Remo was a professional. his assignment was to jump the line to the top. That meant, move into the terrorists' system and kill his way to the top, destroying the system. And his way into the system might be circling the airport at this very moment

Remo honked the horn of the Rolls, a clear, resonant sound that did absolutely nothing to the clog of cars except instigate more horn honking. America. Remo wasn't sure sometimes why Smith was so gung ho to save it. What was even more puzzling was Smith's current strange excitement about the terrorists, even to the point of babbling on an open line. If they were as much a danger as Smith obviously thought, then it was even more important that CURE be careful. More reason to be calm. But then, something had felt wrong with this terrorist business right from the beginning.

ABOUT THE AUTHORS

WARREN MURPHY (1933 – 2015) was born in Jersey City, where he worked in journalism and politics until launching the **Destroyer** series with Richard Sapir in 1971. A screenwriter (*Lethal Weapon II*, *The Eiger Sanction*) as well as a novelist, Murphy's work won a dozen national awards, including multiple Edgars and Shamuses. He was a lecturer at many colleges and universities; his lessons on writing a novel are available on his website, WarrenMurphy.com. A Korean War veteran, some of Murphy's many hobbies included golf, mathematics, opera, and investing. He served on the board of the Mystery Writers of America, and was a member of the Screenwriters Guild, the Private Eye Writers of America, the International Association of Crime Writers, and the American Crime Writers League. He has five children: Deirdre, Megan, Brian, Ardath, and Devin.

RICHARD BEN SAPIR was a New York native who worked as an editor and in public relations, before creating *The Destroyer* series with Warren Murphy. Before his untimely death in 1987, Sapir had also penned a number of thriller and historical mainstream novels, best known of which were *The Far Arena*, *Quest* and *The Body*, the last of which was made recently into a film. The New York Times book review section called him "a brilliant professional."

Made in the USA
San Bernardino, CA
30 January 2019